48 Clicks

By

Theresa J. Gonsalves

ISBN: 978-1-62193-992-4
ISBN 10: 1-62193-992-8
Library of Congress Control Number: 2014945567

Although based on true events, this is a work of fiction.
Any references or similarities to actual events, real people,
living or dead, or to real locales are intended to give the
stories a sense of reality. Any similarity to other names,
characters, places and incidents is coincidental.

TJG Management Publishing Services, Inc.

*"This is a work of fiction. Please don't pick up the shoes and try to
wear them if you know they don't fit. Everything ain't about you." -
Unanimous*

Cast all your anxiety on Him because he cares for you. – 1 Peter 5:7

48 CLICKS
An anthology of three short
stories:
BOUNDARIES,
OBSESSIONS CONTINUED...
and **48 CLICKS!**

*Three captivating stories that are crazy,
funny and sexy and will turn you on with
several unique orgasmic tips to try!*

Content

Acknowledgements

It would be impossible to thank everyone who helped me with this anthology, but a very special thank you goes first to Charlene Fossett, the inspiration behind 48 Clicks! I also thank Tina McKinney for dealing with me unconditionally by not only allowing me to complain about my pain daily as we pray for my new liver, but also for constantly pushing me to keep writing through the pain. She told me to use the pain as a tool, use the emotions to get your words on paper!

I thank my son Todd Love Ball, Jr for stepping up and mending our relationship and encouraging me to move forward. I love you son, I love your wife Kasia and I am completely in love with my more than adorable grandchildren Anya and Dominik. To my son Mychal, I love you… get it together. Tesha Young, my daughter dearest, I love you!

I would also like to thank those who have stood by me continuously supporting my books and our friendships: Lorraine McCollin, Irene Coleman, Kim Coleman, Pamela Lancaster, Vivian Rutherford, Lorelei Lanford, my nieces Monique and Marlene Frye, My niece Brashawna Funderburg, my Goddaughters Danielle Fiers, Krystle Avens and April Washington. If I missed anyone, know that I appreciate all of your loving encouragement.

Sit Back, Relax and Read!

Obsessions Continued...

Prologue

Where Obsessions ends…

Theresa now pitied Vincent and was able to simply let him go. She no longer craved his respect, but would always love him. Now she could actually forgive him. She could smile at the good times they had shared for she knew and would always know that, while Cynthia had his heart, Edna had his body, Theresa had always had his soul!

However, the wrath of Terri still lingered on as Terri vowed, "Vengeance will soon be mine!" For Terri, vengeance had just become her new *obsession!*

….48 clicks begins.

Chapter One

Theresa and Terri were one in the same. But it was clear to most that there were two very distinct personalities. While Theresa was smart, shy, sweet girl next door type who ran her own corporation, Terri couldn't handle heartache and pain and would often act maniacal. Her philosophy questioned why men think they could treat women any way they wanted to with no consequences.

Terri could never get the idea of vengeance out of her head. For as much as she thought she loved Vincent, she often visualized his death. She felt a funeral would serve him much better, especially with the realism of the dream she had of his trying to burn down her house with her and her son in it, nonetheless. Death would be truly final. He also wouldn't be able to hurt any other women as he had done her. There were so many of them and one of them was always willing to take him in.

'Death would have become him', Terri thought. The stages of grief had settled in and she and Theresa had addressed most of them. It felt to them as if he had died anyway.

When she found out about his deception, the first stage of grief she experienced was - the shock and denial: *"No way he was still married to Cynthia, courting some skank named Edna; involved in a swingers club and spending all this time leading me to believe we would get married."*

The second stage was when she became totally numb with disbelief. – *"How could that motherfucker do this to me?!"* Then pain and guilt consumed her – *"It's my fault. Why didn't I see this? Am I that naïve?"* Next came the anger and bargaining – *"I'm going to kill him. Yeah, maybe both of us."* And then there was the stage of depression, reflection and loneliness *"How did I let this man waste so many years of my life?"* she cried, *"Now I will be alone forever."*

Chapter Two

Terri, however, never took the upward turn to simply adjust to life without him, nor did they ever go through the stage of acceptance of what he did. Well, perhaps that would only come once revenge was carried out!

She definitely felt she had to exact some kind of revenge against him and then maybe she would be able to move forward. After all, his actions were intentional. Does he get to waste the most important years of our lives and get to merely walk away? Terri didn't think so.

But what could she do that would really mess him up. He was vain. He was always caught up in what other people thought. The entire Oliver family puts on airs and appearances. Her mind was filled with many crazy thoughts until finally… finally, the light bulb appeared over her head! To make it even better, it was what Theresa had wanted to do all her life. It would be the best revenge of all.

She would write a novel and tell her story to the world!

"A best seller!" she surmised.

She boasted her idea to Vincent, himself, as well as to his best friend, John. They had both continued to entertain conversations with her in order to stay on their toes. They knew what she was capable of, but the distance between Los Angeles and Las Vegas was vast and made her old antics a bit impossible to carry out this time.

Vincent convinced John that she was just talking trash. He didn't take heed to the warning that silence is golden when he hadn't heard from her for four days. He simply felt like her alter personality, Theresa, was coming to her senses and trying to get her life back to normal by accepting what he had done to her.

After all, he thought to himself smugly with a wicked smile, *they,* and there were many, always get over it.

Chapter Three

During the four days of silence, Theresa, along with her alter ego, Terri, managed to write a book she called OBSESSIONS. John was actually the one who came up with the title. Theresa/Terri often wondered why John had been filling her in on what was going on with Vincent. He once said it was because he didn't think it was fair that the others, what should they be called, yes the other victims, that were in Los Angeles, were able to know what was going on while Terri was left out.

John felt that Vincent's instant and complete shut out of Terri was making her more neurotic. During one of their conversations and after going back and forth with Vincent about his actions with Theresa,

John simply concluded, "Both of you are truly obsessed with each other!"

For those four straight days Theresa/Terri wrote with a fervent desire to tell their story and exact her revenge. Writing turned out to be a significant part of the start of her actual healing process as well. She cried for what she herself had started with him by blatantly asking him if he wanted to have an affair. She was brutally honest in telling their story. She even chose to use their real names. How else do you make it real?

There could be no lawsuits if there were no lies. And what other way would she embarrass him and show the world who he truly was if she didn't use their real names. She laughed at the enjoyable times they spent together and she mourned the love that she felt was actually between them. She didn't just disclose his deceit, but she divulged her own stupidities as well. It was a relationship built on a foundation of lies right from the start.

When her manuscript was being edited, with starry eyes, she envisioned people reading Obsessions and could hear their comments echoing loudly throughout her mind, especially from the people who knew him… *"Are you talking about Jack's son? You mean Vincent Oliver from the Chili Factory on Crenshaw?" "No way he could do anything like this." "Those sexy eyes of his made woman crazy for him, of course I can see his acting like that!"*

If they only knew, she snickered as she imagined the reactions and yet here it will be in black and white.

Theresa invested her money and time until finally, OBSESSIONS was hers to share.

The first shipment arrived filling both Theresa/Terri with an abundance of emotions. Writing had always been her dream. She had always been a good writer, but never tried to follow the path. 'Wow!' she cried, feeling exhilarated as she realized his actions actually had forced her to become who she should have been all along.

Theresa could hardly contain her excitement at seeing her first work in print. She shared the news with all of her friends. The ones who read it were in disbelief that she had been so frank.

She had been written about personally in other authors' work and in a gossip magazine about her relationship with Michael

Jackson, but she had never taken the time to write a complete novel of her own. Theresa secretly thanked Vincent for that. Deep down she realized also that she was airing both their dirty laundry and she wondered how her own children would react to it, not to mention the children Vincent had with his wife Cynthia, and probably a few others he wasn't claiming.

She could care less about what Edna thought. Edna was just another side chick. Terri had always felt that Vincent was never too emotionally involved with Edna. She was clearly in his life just for sex.

Before the book was released to the public, Terri sent copies to everyone in Vincent's family. She sent copies to all of his friends whose addresses she had. She even sent copies to Cynthia's subordinates; anyone she could find who was remotely associated with him.

To her surprise, others eagerly sought out the book, including one of his own cousins emailing a request for a copy of the book stating, "I often wondered what my cousin was truly like. I knew no one can be as charming as he appears to be. I want to read this for myself and maybe learn who he really is."

Upon receiving his own copy, John found himself very enthralled in the book. He sat up all night reading it. He called Theresa and said, "Look, I know Vincent is my best friend. He's my boy. But I have to give you your props. You wrote the hell out of that book! I couldn't put it down and I'm not much of a reader. Good job! Damn."

And with that he gave her the address to a couple of their other friends he said wanted to read the book. She was more than happy to oblige and immediately shipped them out.

After a week she spoke to John again, "I got together with the guys and we held a discussion about your book," he informed her.

The general consensus was they felt that even though Vincent was wrong, some of the responsibility of the situation belonged to Cynthia, his wife. She was so into her Holy rolling ways, they concluded, that it allowed him to do whatever he wanted to do. They speculated as to how holy she really was because she didn't want Vincent to see the kid he had with Theresa. What kind of woman, doesn't want a child to have a father? Surely not a woman who claims to be of God? She had the same reaction towards the son he had prior to even meeting him.

They had all sat and discussed their friend. The ones who had known about his relationships outside of his marriage, claimed they had seen it coming. Some of their wives didn't even want their husbands in Vincent's presence. His reputation had definitely preceded him, but now it would be following him in print!

In the company of his friends, Vincent reacted with extreme anger. John actually worried for Theresa's life.

"He has ice running through his veins," John warned her. "I was watching a documentary on Scott Peterson and I noticed they had very similar personality traits. You know who Scott Peterson is don't you? He is the guy who killed his pregnant wife and threw her body in the river just before Christmas. You better be careful."

"In spite of the fact that you just called your best friend a sociopath, I ain't scared of him. Besides, he would be the first suspect. He better hope nothing happens to me." Terri responded laughingly. She put up a brave armor, but held on to slight trepidations. Her guard was definitely up.

Chapter Four

Vincent showed little reaction towards the book to Theresa, but she sure knew he was angry. "I'm not going to read it anyway," he told her, "And you better be prepared because you're going to be sued!"

Terri responded with laughter, "That is exactly what I was hoping for! That will help me draw more attention to the book and increase my sales. Please do. Tell your wife to go ahead. Do it!"

They had bragged about having so much money to use against Theresa in the past. Cynthia's mother had even gone to the extreme of going to the Attorney General to try to get them to press charges against

Theresa for no apparent reason other than she had Cynthia's husband's baby.

"So go for it," Theresa dared, "I'm not the one caught up in what everyone else thinks about me."

"I should have killed your ass when I had the chance..." Vincent responded unintentionally.

A slight shiver of fear tingled throughout her body. She brushed it aside, "You're too much of a wimp to do anything idiot," she retorted continuing to push his buttons.

With the help of a friend and his marketing idea, immediate sales were surprisingly fabulous. She ordered five thousand copies of her book and they sold quickly. She had gotten revenge and put a few bucks in her pocket.

Some of her clients questioned her sanity after reading some of the stuff that she had done, however, she did good accounting work and they could clearly see the separation of the two egos that flourished within her.

After two months passed and although Terri still harassed Vincent, she had actually been quieting down. Her satisfaction came from time to time as she received emails from quite a few women asking if her book was really true....'Absolutely' would be her honest response. She explained to them that she had hoped in reading this book if they saw themselves in a similar relationship that they would be smart enough to get out. There were of course calls from women calling her the ultimate bitch and saying Vincent didn't deserve to be treated this way. Probably some of his additional side chicks or his family.

"Whatever" Terri responded with indifference.

Theresa was ultimately surprised when she received a phone call from a woman identifying herself as Jamal's mother. She had refused to give her name. Jamal was Vincent's first son. She just wanted to know what was in the book about them and had wanted to make sure it wouldn't affect her son who was doing very well in the U.S. Air Force.

All Terri would say to her was "Read the book. It's available on Amazon." She had no beef with this woman who mentioned it was Vincent's cousin who had told her about Obsessions.

Edna had called screaming and threatening to sue as well. "Edna, you overestimated Vincent's feelings towards you and since you want him back, you know he would be very upset if you do anything to hurt me." Terri was cracking up. She did everything she could to keep her self-control and undermine Edna's beliefs. Vincent had shut her out completely. It was easy to just tell her anything.

Chapter Five

All had been quiet for a couple of months when Theresa's doorbell rang. It was early evening and she wasn't expecting any company. She was home alone.

"Who is it?" she asked as she looked through the peephole. She saw him at the same time he responded.

"Vince."

Without fear, she opened the door.

"Come on in," she said as she walked away leading him into her office. He followed her in and stood against the wall, making sure he didn't get too comfortable.

He had come unannounced. He didn't give her any opportunity to tell anyone that he was visiting, yet she felt no fear from him. But still what did he want?

"What do you want? Why are you here?" she asked.

She was certain he hadn't come here for some great proclamation of his love or even to see their son.

She looked him up and down as if he was a brand new Mercedes Benz and she was inspecting it. He looked good as he always did. She soaked in his scent. Her heart beat wildly. "Calm yourself down girl," she told herself.

"I need you to stop selling that book," he pleaded.

"You have to be kidding me," Terri said with great satisfaction doing everything in her power to keep from laughing. "Why?"

"It's affecting my son. You said you wouldn't do anything to let the kids get hurt."

Apparently, his older son Vince Jr. had been getting flack about the book at the college he was attending. He was on the UC Davis basketball team and though not sure how, the book had been spread to the team. Jokes about his mama, his daddy and his daddy's side chicks were affecting his game.

"You have to be out of your fucking mind to even ask me that? You never tried to protect the kid I have with you! You are fucking crazy!" she responded with great irritability. "You have some nerve putting your lips together to even utter those words to me. I feel bad for your son, but it's not my problem."

"Well, how about if I buy the rights from you?" he offered.

Again, Terri snickered, but was impressed that he had learned the language of the book world.

"Show me the money! How much?" She wanted to jump up and down, mimicking that infamous scene from Jerry Maguire. She held her composure.

"Fifty thousand," he proposed.

"You make no effort to even see Mychal, yet you have the audacity to come here and make that offer so your *other* son won't be embarrassed. Fuck you."

"What will it take?" he begged.

"Nothing. I make no deals with the devil I am looking at in front of me. Are we done?"

Terri got up and walked him to the front door and opened it for him to leave. Theresa, however, wanted to take his hand and take him back to her bedroom so he could fuck her. She was clearly missing the Magic. The magic actually had become the essence of their relationship. She loved him, but she hadn't actually liked him for quite some time. He still looked good though.

"It was nice seeing you," she said halfheartedly.

"Think about it…." he responded, "I am truly sorry for what I did to you."

"Yeah right," she said sarcastically as she shut the door.

She was still unable to accept that he was over her. Bastard! Thank you for bringing out the writer in me.

Three years later, Theresa released her second book, The Man in the Woods.

Chapter Six

(In the year of 2008)

Theresa zoomed to Los Angeles the minute, Tesha, her daughter, called and said she was in labor. It was only a five hour drive and Tesha was just heading on her way to the hospital. When Tesha called, Theresa had to be there. Since Tesha's real mom had passed, Theresa had stepped in. The thought of having her second child without her mom was devastating. So she expected her 'mom' Theresa to step in.

After Jacob's birth and preferring privacy, Theresa got a room at the Embassy Suites in El Segundo. Once alone and exhausted, she couldn't help but pick up the telephone and call Vincent. This was Los Angeles, their old stomping grounds. This was where it all began with him. It seemed unnatural to be there and not talk to him.

Vincent saw her number on his caller ID as his phone rang seemingly with an urgency. He hesitated about picking it up. He justified answering by reminding himself that they do have a kid together.

"Hey, what's up?" he answered.

"Don't you have another way of answering the phone," Terri asked immediately annoyed with the same old greeting. Some things hadn't changed in over 20 years.

"What do you want?" he retorted himself, instantly agitated, but as usual intrigued with her gall. This girl had more balls than most of the guys he knew.

"I'm in town at the Embassy Suites in El Segundo. I want you to come over and spend the night with me."

"What are you doing here?"

"Tesha had her baby. She wanted me to be here."

"Tell her congratulations."

"Sure, I'll tell her. So are you coming?"

"What makes you think I want to see you?"

"Well, you still love me," she replied confidently, "I haven't been with anyone else and I could use some face."

Vincent laughed a very hearty laugh as if she had just told him a really good joke.

"Quit wasting time Vincent," Theresa told him, "You know you are going to come."

"Are you sure?"

"Yes. I left a key for you at the front desk."

"I'll think about it, but I doubt it."

"You know that fantasy I always had about your waking me up with some face? Make it come true for me," she teased unaware that she had already made his dick rise.

"Whatever Terri. Goodbye." He hung up with a smile.

She hung up and took a shower. Everything within her believed that he would show up. After two hours passed, she resigned herself to accept that maybe he wasn't going to come after all. She drifted off to sleep.

An hour later she heard the door opening. She pretended to remain asleep. She felt him softly get on the bed and pull the sheet down off of her. He lifted her nightgown above her waist and put his tongue gently on her clitoris and began to lick slowly.

Unable to keep pretending to be asleep, a moan escaped her lips. He stopped and got up. She wanted to grab his head and put it back where it belonged. He was just getting started. She wanted him to continue and finish.

Light tension filled the room. "You knew I would come," he said.

They held each other's gaze as he took off his clothes and headed towards the shower. A slight awkwardness overcame her as the sound of the shower running awakened her further. This is *wrong*, she thought.

"Damn it! Why can't I stay away from her," he muttered to himself drying himself off as he headed towards the bed. Seconds later, his mouth was upon hers. Warm lips molded over hers as one hand reached low and spread over the curve of her spine. She did nothing to stop him or to alleviate the onslaught of mixed feelings to her sanity.

Instead, she closed her eyes and felt the wonder of his mouth and the heat of his body against hers.

How long had it been since she had kissed him? Made love to him? She closed her mind to that train of thought and lost herself in the moment, feeling the pressure of his lips against hers and the weight of his body as he rolled over her. His tongue slid easily through her mouth, the tip touching the ridges along the roof as he tasted her, touched her. She kissed him back, her own tongue exploring the mouth of this man who had crushed her heart and infuriated her half to death.

Don't trust this shit, Theresa thought. It's nothing. Two idiotic horny people caught together in the middle of a long dark night. This isn't what you want she said to herself. But she couldn't stop. She wouldn't stop.

Where Vincent was concerned, there was no rational or sane side to her behavior. But tonight this loving was long overdue and she desperately needed some release.

Tonight, this was not a thoughtful joining. This was not a loving exploration. This was a fierce coupling driven by need.

He twisted her nightgown over her hips. His fingertips skimmed her body, his palms caressing. She had trouble taking a breath and couldn't think. She could only feel.

He caressed every part of her body within reach as he slowly managed to get the gown off. He lingered as low moans continued to escape her lips as he lightly tickled her ribs with his fingertips teasing and touching as her nipples tightened so much they ached.

Her wetness was fluid and before she could wonder if he was going to do the Magic, that helped to bind her to him so submissively, he lowered himself down between her legs. "Is this what you want?" he teased.

"Shut up and just do it," Theresa moaned. Vincent obliged. He knew this drove her crazy. *Slowly he crooked his index finger on his right hand and inserted it in her vagina behind her clitoris to her G spot. He had long, sleek fingers which enabled him to go in so deeply. It had taken him a while to conquer this, but after numerous tries, and with several women, he thought to himself, he was able to perfect this. He slowly rubbed the G spot as Theresa squirmed, "What are you doing to me? What the fuck are you doing to me?"*

She could barely withstand the intensity. Yet she begged for it whenever she could. She tensed further in delicious agony as he then put his tongue on her clitoris as she spread eagle holding it open for him to get direct contact. He tasted her slowly, then swiftly until suddenly that explosion he missed so much erupted like that of a man discharging his own. He loved it when she came. No other woman he had could come like that.

He lightened up a little and as she caught up on her breathing, he stuck his tongue back onto the clitoris licking as hard and fast as he could. A second spasm hit her hard until she pleaded with him to stop.

She wanted to turn over and go to sleep, but knew she had to let him have his as well. "Your turn," she whispered. He lifted himself giving her more access to the warmth emanating between his legs. She gently grabbed his rock hard penis and guided it into her soaking wet vagina..."Watch out!" he whispered playfully, "that's dangerous territory." He plunged in with deep, swift thrusts and swore as his body stiffened. He slammed his eyes shut as he tried to hold on as long as he could. Quivering, he thrust faster and wilder until his entire body collapsed in ecstasy.

He initially wanted to roll over and just go to sleep, but he had truly missed her and he wanted to talk. He wanted to relish in the comfort they use to share with just simple conversation. He wanted to feel that closeness again.

"Everything had been so simple between us," he commented aloud.

Theresa chose not to get angry at the stupidity of his words. Yes of course they had been simple for him. He truly had his cake and definitely ate it too. *Literally.*

She brushed his words aside as she tried to drift off to sleep. Why bother arguing? She would just be fighting for something that would never be.

"Are you divorced yet?" Theresa asked him.

"Yes. You can do what you do and check it out online if you don't believe me, but yes I am divorced."

"Hmph! Imagine that!" she said sarcastically. "I've been with you since 1986 and here it is 2008. This is the first time I have been with you as a single man. And now that you are single, I can't be with you."

"Well, if only you reacted differently..." His words ran off.

"Shut up Vincent," Theresa said softly spooning her body into his. She didn't want this evening to turn into a battle of what ifs. She didn't want to get angry. She just wanted to relish in the moment of being in his arms once again.

His scent alone could arouse her and this time was no different. "Ready for another round?" she asked him.

They made love again. This time it was consumed with tenderness and warmth. He held her in his arms the rest of the night. He didn't want to let her go, but he didn't know how to forgive her for what she did to him. It wasn't really just about his forgiveness. How could he bring her to family functions after all that had happened?

They parted with loving kisses and warm smiles.

"I miss you," he told her.

Chapter Seven

(In the year of 2010)

Theresa and Vincent hadn't seen each other in over two years. He paid his child support, but wasn't pro-active in their son's life at all. He did actually take Mychal for a month when Theresa and Mychal started having issues, other than that, he merely felt sending a check was good enough.

In October of 2010, Vincent still proved he had feelings for her, when she showed up in Los Angeles and had a faux pas with her debit card. She was hosting a Michael Jackson pajama party weekend in honor of Michael's life. She needed money and Vincent was the only one she could call.

It was wonderful of him to show up and give her more money than she needed to continue the trip she had set up for her and the MJ girls. He looked good and she could feel herself get wet as he pulled up in what appeared to be a brand new Cadillac 300.

The girls eyed him. They knew their history. Hell, they had read Obsessions too, and they all wanted to get a glimpse of him. Even though he had caused Theresa some major heartache, once they saw him, all eyes were on him.

"He is fine!" They all agreed. They also figured the love was still there. He was coming to her rescue, not just hers, but also theirs! So once again, he looked like the hero.

Theresa smiled at him as he handed her the cash and he smiled back. His dick was getting hard just looking at her. It didn't matter what they had gone through, she always had that impact on him. Before the girls could get to the car to be introduced, she whispered, "Damn, I wish I could just fuck your brains out right now." She turned around and found Danielle right over her shoulders. Danielle smiled. She had heard, but wouldn't say a word. Theresa introduced the girls to him. She whispered, "Sorry I don't have time to meet up with you this time."

He looked into her eyes and with his eyes said, "I still love you."

She knew he did. Their feelings were mutual. I love you, but I hate your fucking ass too.

Chapter Eight

(In the year of 2011)

Theresa was in a sound sleep in Lorraine's king size bed when the sound of her phone ringing woke her up. She had flown in from Las Vegas to Boston and arrived around 2 a.m. She was exhausted. She squinted to look at the number, but didn't recognize it. It didn't matter, she would answer it anyway.

Today she had an appearance at Frugal's book store in Roxbury, MA. Later in the evening she was having a book release party. This was her first kids' book titled, Eating Gavin's Way. She was proud of it, but more importantly, she was home in Boston, with family and friends to share in this event.

A lot of her classmates from high school who knew of her writing passion would be there to support her.

She picked up the phone.

"Hello…" she answered, her voice very groggy.

"Hello Theresa. This is Edna," said the other voice on the phone with vagueness.

Neither Theresa nor Terri had any recollection of the name.

"Who?" she asked puzzled.

"Edna."

"Who?" Theresa asked again still not recognizing the name or voice.

"I know you remember me," she said unwaveringly.

Theresa truly didn't have a clue.

"I don't know who you are," she said now annoyed as well as embarrassed, as this girl clearly seemed to know who she was.

"Vince." Edna stated.

"Ohhh…..*Edna!*" Terri said in total surprise. Vincent's side chick. "Why the hell are you calling me? It's been seven years! I'm sure you are over this bullshit by now."

"I called because your book is still causing me problems," she replied.

"What?! Girl, like I said, it's been seven years. What do you want?" Theresa's irritation was apparent.

Edna had to regroup. She totally expected Theresa to easily remember her no matter how much time had elapsed. She figured, 'Hell, if I made it in her book, she should definitely remember me!'

Edna continued, "Well, I went on a job interview and there on the girl's desk sat a copy of Obsessions. When the girl realized I was the Edna in the book, I didn't get the job."

"First off," laughed Terri. "You probably did a lousy interview. Your name is too common for anyone to just recognize that you are the person in the book. Come on now 'Edna Williams', even if you Google that name you would come up with quite a few hits that have no relevance to you. So unless you told her specifically that it was you in the book, then she wouldn't have known. But hey, I am glad to hear that people are reading the book seven years later."

Still thrown off guard, Edna hesitated. She started reminiscing about the situation between herself, Vincent and Theresa. Why would Vincent even tell his little Vegas bitch about our sexcapades we shared in the first place? He said she was just his Vegas bitch and when he talked about their son, he never called him by his name, just always said, *'the boy'*. And now this bitch didn't even remember me.

"Well, I was wondering if you could take my name off of your websites?" Edna asked timidly, her mind still wandering.

"Your name isn't on any of my websites any more Edna. I took all that down," Theresa responded. "Is that it?" She didn't want to be on the phone with this girl any longer than necessary.

"Yes, it's still on one. Can you look it up and take it off?" she pleaded.

"Hang on Edna. Let me get my laptop and look up what you are talking about."

"Sure," Edna said as agreeably as possible. If this book truly was affecting her, she didn't want her name affiliated with it anymore and this was the only site she saw it on. If I am nice to this bitch, she will take it off.

As she held the phone, patiently waiting for Theresa to return, her mind continued to wander back to her sex life with Vincent and what they shared with another couple they had met in a swingers group.

Edna had loved Vincent as much as Theresa had perhaps. But for him he had met his sexual match. Vincent's feelings weren't the same. He didn't mind sharing Edna with other people. Theresa was all his and he knew it. He couldn't fathom the thought of another dick in Theresa.

Edna, on the other hand, felt Theresa just didn't give it to him sexually the right way. In fact, she had clearly told Theresa that her problem with Vincent was she couldn't satisfy him the way she had.

Edna and Vincent had taken their sexual appetites to the Shades of Gray level. Switching, swapping, sharing... whatever you want to call it. It wasn't until she read Obsessions that she found out Theresa had actually tricked *her* into giving her the information about their sex life. 'The little trick,' smirked Edna. But Edna knew she sure blew Theresa's mind when she told her about Vincent having experimented with men. He sure tried to talk himself out of that one, Edna laughed to herself, but I am sure Theresa believed it. After all, Theresa herself manipulated him into getting her pregnant when she tried that butt plug on his ass that apparently he liked so much. Edna started laughing out loud as she visualized Vincent with a butt plug sticking out his ass! She was still laughing when Theresa came back to the phone.

They went through the motions of finding where she was still mentioned on one of Theresa's websites. Theresa kindly removed it. Edna was surprised. Maybe Theresa was actually over him.

"Oh, by the way, how is Vincent doing?" Edna asked.

"I don't know. I don't talk to him."

"Come on. You must talk to him. You have a kid together. I heard he has prostate cancer. Is that right?"

"Actually, I don't know. I really don't talk to him much. I didn't know that," Theresa responded with nonchalance.

"Yeah, I heard he looks horrible. People say he isn't doing well and he has gotten really skinny."

"Oh well, I guess that's his issue." Theresa said, "I imagine I will find out sooner or later. Thanks for telling me. Is there anything else you need?"

"No, but I just want you to know I follow you and I see all you are doing on Facebook."

"Whatever floats your boat Edna. My life is an open book as you may notice," Terri laughed, "Oh, and just so you know, as far as you are concerned, I don't even think about you." She hung up the phone.

The phone call had actually annoyed the hell out of Theresa. She was again reminded of Vincent's unwarranted deceit, especially with Edna having been the one who told her about Vincent's experimenting with men.

The visual was instant. Theresa had personally read about Vincent and Edna toying around with a couple they met at a swingers club called Lifestyles. She had broken into Vincent's email and read the back and forth communication.

Thomas and Carol were Edna and Vincent's third couple to try to swing with. Carol often was referred to as Passion and Thomas was known as Dragon because he had an extremely large penis for a white man. His dick intimidated most women, let alone men. Caught up in the moment after watching Edna and Carol get off so pugnaciously together, Vincent and Dragon wanted to top them.

Dragon was going to be the rider. They had already been warming up with rough saturating kisses and Dragon had been wetting Vincent's anal opening with a light KY jelly moisturizer. Vincent squirmed in anticipation and delight.

Dragon decided it would be gentler to go into him in a spooned position instead of on all fours. Vincent had told him it was his first time with a man, but with his lack of humility, Dragon doubted that. He would still tread lightly. As he fondled and tweaked Vincent's nipples with a pinching sensation, Vincent bucked his ass back towards Dragon anxiously wanting to feel what Dragon had to offer. Dragon took his time, slowly teasing him, wanting to hear this 'virgin' man beg him to stick it in. He paced himself. He didn't want to hurt him. He kissed and licked along the back of his neck and behind his ears and when Dragon put his dragonius tongue into Vincent's ear, Vincent began begging him to enter.

Dragon stuck his penis into Vincent's anus, gently gliding it in slowly. He had entered about an inch in and moved with gentle strokes. And with just those few gentle strokes, Vincent came rather quickly with the strongest orgasm he had ever experienced. As Carol and Edna watched, Edna found herself overcome with extreme jealousy and it made her wonder. She kept her poise as she realized he had never come that strongly with her.

Dragon, while disappointed that Vincent had come so fast, easily released himself. He wanted to ram it in hard at the excitement of Vincent's orgasm and screams, but remained steadfast in not wanting to hurt him. He wanted to be able to do this again.

After getting nauseous, Theresa shook the visual out of her mind's eyes and immediately called Vincent. After their common 'hello' courtesies, she told him about Edna's call.

"Why in the hell is your girlfriend calling me after seven years? She told me you had prostate cancer. Is that true?"

Vincent without denying or confirming the cancer allegation simply replied, "I'm all right."

"Look, Vincent, if you have some kind of prostate cancer or colon cancer, you really should let us know because we do have a son and he would need to know that information. You do realize that shit is partly hereditary don't you?"

"I'm all right," is all he ignorantly continued to reply to the question. "Asshole," Terri thought to herself. "But hey, you picked him…"

"Well, why is your girlfriend calling me? She was talking about Obsessions is affecting her life. It's been seven damn years."

Vincent chuckled and revealed that Edna had called him too after not having communicated with her in a few years. She had told him that her boyfriend, Tony, had read Obsessions and after reading about their swapping endeavors, he broke off their relationship. Now they were embroiled in restraining orders and lawsuits because Tony now believed Edna gave him venereal warts. Tony had even had the audacity to call Vincent and make threats.

Vincent informed Tony he wanted nothing to do with Edna and all that stuff had happened several years earlier and he was done with her back then. Yet again Vincent had been noncommittal in giving any information to Tony about their sexual antics.

"Edna is just as fucking crazy as you are," he told Terri, "In fact, she may just have you beat."

Tired of hearing his voice and listening to his stupidity, Theresa just simply hung up the phone. Vincent hated when she just hung up in his face. It perturbed him to no end. He called her back. She didn't bother answering.

Vincent slammed his phone shut as he walked angrily into the oncologist office. He certainly didn't need her adding to his stress at this time.

Chapter Nine

(In the year of 2013)

Theresa knew she wouldn't be coming back to Los Angeles for a while. The sadness of Michael Jackson's death still haunted her. It was another year and she was still in disbelief that he was actually gone.

The air was heavy, but the sun still warmed the day. She was ready to head back to Scottsdale and continue moving on with her life. She was ready to start looking for love again and pursue her dream of becoming a bestselling author.

Theresa stood in the window of the Sheraton Four Points Hotel over by LAX. Los Angeles held other ghost for Theresa as well and she was waiting for the shadowing arrival of this one.

She watched hoping to see him cross the street. It had been at least four years since they engaged in any intimacies.

Even after what one would believe was their ending Theresa and Vincent had managed to still get together for random opportunities. According to Vincent, he was now divorced. Theresa never checked. She didn't really care any longer. She no longer wanted to be with him. Her alter ego Terri still craved vengeance. Theresa simply wanted to satisfy the cravings he brought about. She continued to miss the magic. It was going on ten years and she still hadn't been able to share herself with another man. It had been at least four years since they had been together. They had still communicated from time to time, even teasingly, with text messages.

Vincent in denying himself to Theresa also considered himself punishing her. "What prize did he think he really was?" Terri would often wonder. She would laugh at some of the stupid things he would say to her. "If only you had been patient, we could have been together."

"If only you had been a real man," Terri would taunt back. Terri was always cautious.

Theresa didn't see Vincent cross the street but she could feel him in her body. It was funny how she started getting wet just sensing he was close.

Her body always betrayed her where he was concerned. She smiled, knowing he would be knocking at the door momentarily. Her senses were still very much alive with him, as suddenly, as was anticipated, there was a light knock on the door.

Vincent stood at the door. Instant nerves set in with Theresa. She was almost shaking, but yet the comfort of him was still there. He looked damn good as he always did. His scent, as in the past, intoxicated her, making her want to immediately remove all her clothes and lay herself across the bed and scream, "TAKE ME DAMMIT!"

His hair had thinned out quite a bit. Theresa had just cut all her hair off the day before.

"You look so cute," he smiled, "the haircut fits you." Theresa just smiled back at him. They made small chit chat. Theresa nervously walked around him in circles. Finally, he grabbed her and kissed her.

"It's like this animal magnetism…" he exclaimed, "Whenever I am near you, I just want you. That will never go away."

He kissed her again as the clothes began to come off and they fell onto the bed. With a moan, she touched the strong muscles of his shoulders and arms. Her small fingers brushed his skin causing the flesh to tighten.

"Careful," he warned as she glided her hands across his abdomen and along his hips. "Never, " she said as she kissed him with wild abandonment.   It had been so long. He touched her everywhere, kissing her and delving in with his tongue, into her clitoris as she reached down, holding it open for him as she used to. Theresa came fast and furious.

Four years was a long time to be without it. Yet it wasn't the magic she longed for.

To anticipate the magic right away was asking for too much and she didn't even think she could handle it. She settled for the multiple orgasms until he pulled upward into her arms. Holding her fast beneath him, he levered himself up on his elbows and looking into her eyes, he slid her knees farther apart with his own. She gasped as he hovered over her and waited. She bit her bottom lip in anticipation. But he didn't move. He stared down at her, feeling the heat between them.

She whispered anxiously to him, "Vince, why aren't you coming in?" His devilish smile stretched wide "In time..." he teased. She looked at him quizzically as he smoothed her short hair. His hands trembled. "I've always loved you," he said, his voice harsh with sincerity as he finally thrust deep inside her. "Damn it all to hell!" he exclaimed, "I really do love you."

His orgasm was quick but the thrusts were painful. Theresa did not anticipate this intense pain. It was like a stick stabbing along her insides. She didn't understand it. She held up her legs as her vagina sucked in his penis to quickly bring him to as swift an orgasm as possible.

"So I slept with him yet again...she thought. So what? No big deal right? Then why did it feel so massive as if her life had shifted on its axis?

"Oh for Christ sakes, stop sounding like some starry eyed heroine in a Danielle Steele novel," she cautioned herself.

She rolled over. He was lying on his stomach, arms folded under his squashed pillow, his head twisted in her direction. The sheets were tangled over his buttocks. He slept soundly snoring softly, his face relaxed, his light brown skin a contrast to the white sheets. Her heart filled at the sight of him. He was just taking a quick nap. She watched him in bewilderment and thought about the pain.

After a while, with a sleepy groan, he rolled onto his back. His entire body became exposed. His erection quite evident.

"Getting an eyeful?" he asked as her eyes gazed straight at his hardness. A heat wave crawled up the back of her neck. "Like what you see?"

"You are hopeless," she laughed.

"Ahhh, I love it when you talk dirty to me!" he said playfully as he rolled over to her stark naked just as she was. He wrapped his arms around her. He slid his tongue over her teeth and deep into her mouth.

Still kissing her he stood them both up and walked her backwards into the shower. As the water temperature heated so did she. Her pussy pounded as his hand moved across her body.

Using a bar of soap and wash cloth, he gently washed her, kissed her and pinned her against the tiles lifting her onto his thick throbbing erection sliding her easily onto him as the water cascaded over them.

"Oh God..." He groaned out loud, then shuddered a release. He threw his head back. The cords of his neck distended as he came inside her, stiffening, every muscle in his body contracting. She was eye level with him staring deep into his smoky eyes.

"You're incredible, " he said.

She laughed, "Uh, you did all the work!"

Theresa played along to make sure he was satisfied, after all, lovemaking, between them was always a two way thing, but she still felt something just wasn't right. The stabbing pain wasn't as bad in that position, but why the pain. She couldn't figure it out.

For a moment she thought that perhaps it was because it had been so long for her, but no, this was different. This was real pain. She would just go with the flow. This wasn't one of their fabulous sex romps, but she would humor him nonetheless. He always thought he was on the money. She would ponder what the hell the problem was.

As she lay in his arms, she asked, "So what's your story these days? Are you in a committed relationship?"

"I date," he answered, shrugging his shoulders. She had heard rumor that he supposedly lived with some woman. He still couldn't remain faithful.

And once again he ran that line by her, "If you didn't react as you did, we could be together." And again, she thought to herself, 'Oh no, only Cynthia could claim this prize he thinks he is. Yeah, the sex was good. Maybe he lost that mojo at this point. At least with me.' She just couldn't quite pinpoint the problem.

They said their goodbyes to each other. She would let him think that this was another great 'fuck' between them.

He passionately kissed her goodbye. He was in his usual rush, as with most of their previous romps.

Who the hell was he rushing to get back to, she wondered, or where. Theresa chose to just look at it as it was. Another frolic in the hay. She was always comfortable with him and hadn't been with anyone other than him since they first met in 1986.

As soon as he left, she followed out the door behind him to head back to Scottsdale, AZ. She was exhausted. It would be a long six hour drive.

Chapter Ten

Theresa constantly thought about what the nature of the pain was she had experienced during their last sexual encounter. She was baffled and couldn't get it out of her head.

They had been sending sexy text messages back and forth to each other since their last tryst.

On his birthday, July 13th, Theresa wanted to treat him to a sexual visual of self-masturbation. He would love that she thought.

"You woke her up and now she craves more," Theresa wrote. "Calling your name as I do it myself," she told him as she slowly rubbed her breasts. She had her personal warming gel ready so she could show him her clitoral and vaginal masturbation.

"You want to watch on FaceTime?" she teased.

"Trying not to think about it," he responded, "As usual, I belong to others."

"What the fuck do the others have to do with anything?" Terri texted back her anger rising. She was bewildered. Was he getting caught up and trying to push her off a little bit? "Where the hell did that come from?"

"You know I go straight to your soul," Vincent crooned as if he was actually singing a song.

"I was in control. I was simply taking it as it was. But you just ruined it so this is not something I want to do any more." He had killed the mood.

"I told you I was dating."

"Dating is different than married or committed." Theresa was trying to be rational, not allowing Terri to surface in anger. Where was this coming from?

"But since you said that, you just ruined our fun, so thanks for the moment. I wish you continued success in your womanly endeavors. I can keep blocking the cravings."

"Don't hang up," he squirmed, "Notice, I said 'trying to not think' about you. There is no denying our chemistry. There's just too much history."

Here we go again thought Terri. "I know with you love doesn't trump history and age doesn't seem to bring you any wisdom in change. I guess that is just the sociopath in you." She was now truly annoyed.

They stopped texting.

Two days later he texted her, "The last thing in the world I want to do is hurt you. You get even and more!"

"I have a little more self-worth now. And I can still hear you saying the 'you should have been patient' line which is ridiculous," she responded back, "What the hell did you expect me to do when you had my complete trust and then I start hearing about Edna, Cynthia and then even a *man*."

"I will give you the outing me. I deserved that. It's all the extra stuff that came after. Like Obsessions, I mean, for Christ sakes, I kept coming back. I just hoped you had a little vision and foresight to see that once all this blew over, I would come back. I deserved your outing me and more. But you made it hard for me to come back this time after all was said and done. But yet here we are again."

"That's just it Vincent. We are nowhere. Just a little sex. I have moved on mentally, just not physically. I still crave you," Theresa wrote sadly.

Terri felt proud.

Chapter Eleven

Three months had gone by and Theresa *still* wondered what caused that pain she experienced during their last sexual rendezvous. Something just wasn't quite right.

The answer slowly crept upon her. The dawn was awakened. Though he refused to answer her question relative to having cancer, she knew Edna hadn't made that up. His hair was balding, yes age would do that, but so would chemotherapy and radiation.

He was skinnier than she had ever seen him. And when they were in the hotel room the last time, he had told her that when he changed his eating habits, even Jack, his father, thought he was sick because he had lost so much weight. It had sounded like a justification for his being so skinny.

She hadn't even asked him about it, although Theresa's eyes told her otherwise. He was trying to justify things and not let her know about the cancer. He did have prostate cancer. She suspected he was now cancer free, thankfully, but finally the answer had come to her.

After treatment for prostate cancer, a lot of time, men are unable to have real orgasms or they get replacement parts. He would only be able to have dry orgasms. He would have a hard time remaining erect.

She thought back to how long it took him to consummate their reunion the last time they were together. Wait a minute, she wondered, was he taking the time to pump it up?

"Oh my God! He has a fake dick!" Terri cackled aloud like a wicked witch. "Vengeance is mine said the Lord!" She shouted and stomped her feet.

What irony. The tool he used to manipulate and use all these women was affected by his treatment to survive and now he has a fake penis!

Theresa did some research and talked to a friend of hers whose husband had a prosthetic penis. She described the first time having sex with his using the prosthetic included that same stabbing like pain. She never tried it again. She recalled his having to use a pump that was implanted in his side to pump it up.

Oh my God… serves him right. What a *just* punishment.

Terri wasn't so heartless that she would be jumping for joy over his cancer. She was falling out hysterically over the satisfaction of the punishment. This was for every girl he ever fucked over, every heart he ever broke, every spirit he ever killed!

This mother fucker has a fake penis!!!!

Theresa had to contain Terri's joy. She was literally in hysterics. "Hey Vincent!" She shouted into the air! "I heard it takes 48 clicks to pump up your fake dick!" She couldn't contain herself. She held her bike pump in the air, "Here you go sir, just push down and pump!"

She definitely wanted to make sure Vincent was aware that she knew. She sent him a text.

"By the way, I could tell the difference!"

He instantly knew that she had figured it out. She would definitely have been the one to get it.

His response was immediate, "Difference?"

"Hmmm...yes think about it?" Terri was ROFLOL (rolling on the floor laughing out loud).

"Better or not better," Vincent texted back.

"Not better," she responded, "Different. Maybe we should try it again."

"Ha ha ha! Nice try." He texted back with a laughing smiley face.

"Maybe, I should have rephrased that last line differently," she responded. "If you wanted to seriously know, we can discuss it. I don't feel as if you value my thoughts and opinions. After all, we only fucked for 20 years."

He picked up the telephone and called her. For Theresa, that was total confirmation. He realized she truly had figured it out. None of the others had.

She wasn't ready however for this conversation. How could she talk to him without saying it serves you right? You got what you deserved.

"Hey, I am tired and grouchy. Can we discuss this later?"

"Sure..." Vincent said. He was thrown off. She always took his calls.

After she hung up, she texted him.

"When you had cancer, didn't you feel like you should live life after you survived it? Perhaps *live* life and not be so caught up in what everyone else thinks?"

Vincent didn't respond.

Terri on the other hand was satisfied with the results and a couple of days later she called and left him a message starting off by singing, "Pump it up! Pump it up! Pump it up home boy, just like that!"

"Hey Vincent! How many licks does it take to get to the end of a Tootsie roll pop! No! No! No! That should be how many clicks does it take to inflate your fake ass dick! Forty eight!" she shouted...."Forty Eight!"

As Vincent listened to the message, his ego deflated. He had realized his life with women would never be the same. Ever since he had read the book, The Sensuous Woman, when he was younger, he had become obsessed with pleasing women sexually.

Yet he never looked out for their hearts. He never truly cared. Yes, his punishment was harsh, but deserved.

Theresa put on some Babyface music. She played her favorite song, Where Will You Go. It had always reminded her of Vincent. She poured herself a glass of CASA Rossa Rivata wine. She raised her glass, "Here's to you Vincent," she said softly. *Click!*

Her forgiveness was real.

Terri was nowhere to be found.

BOUNDARIES

Crossing the lines

Chapter One

Sad eyes highlighted the beautiful smile of Yanique Lacroix. Her five foot, three inch stature at one hundred and ten pounds was slender and graceful.

A transport from Haiti to the United States, she resided in Boston, MA. A large Haitian community embraced most of the Hyde Park area of Boston. Yanique was a light brown skinned woman, skinny but not the typical beautiful French Creole woman as most of them were often considered. Long black hair sat on her shoulders, accompanied by a crooked nose which had always been the topic of her being teased while growing up in Haiti.

Yanique was always the girl that was left out. Instead of being the envy of most of the Haitian girls, she was the joke of them all. When her mother moved her and her sisters to the United States, Yanique felt that the move would make things quite different for her. Instead, it got worse. For most of her high school years, she retreated to within herself, living in a world of fantasy and isolation.

Her mother, Nadeige Lacroix often told her she should put voodoo on those kids who constantly teased her. Nadeige practiced voodoo as a religion while in Haiti and carried her beliefs with her. The teachings didn't go along with the beliefs of the typical religions in the States, so her children simply just dismissed her teachings. Nadeige would often try to teach her daughters love spells to make sure they would capture the right man.

By the age of thirty-two, Yanique found herself through several relationships that had resulted in three separate pregnancies, from three different men, all who had treated her poorly.

When she found herself pregnant with yet a fourth baby and again another no good man who didn't want her to have the baby, she decided to give in to an abortion this time. It was against all that was inside of her, but she felt there was no way she could handle another pregnancy on her own.

It was wonderful to have the support of her mother who took up the responsibilities of her other children's dead beat absent fathers. Her mother was aging and she couldn't possibly impose another child on her.

Off she went solemnly to the abortion clinic. Since she was receiving sedation, she had to take public transportation there. She boarded the bus heading toward the orange train line that would take her to the Planned Parenthood facility in Jamaica Plain. She could imagine hearing the condescending tones of people asking her why she didn't use birth control. *'You already have three kids.'* Who did they think they were to judge her?

She didn't want the scrutiny of her so called friends who would just talk about her behind her back. She held her head down as she walked by a group of people with picket signs that said, 'Women do Regret Abortion' and 'Abortion Kills Children'.

A woman tried to hand her a pamphlet. She pushed her imposing hand away from her. A security guard came down the steps to escort her in.

Yanique filled out the appropriate paperwork to allow the doctors to suck this baby out of her. She was led into an exam room where she was instructed to take her clothes off and was given a paper gown to put on.

She laid up on the table in the cold environment of the sterile abortion facility, her legs wide open in the stirrups with a white paper cloth draped over her legs. A rather large nurse walked in, picked up the clipboard to review her paperwork and smiled at her. "Are you sure this is what you want to do honey?" Yanique shook her head affirmatively and quickly turned her head in shame, wanting to be invisible.

She looked around the small room for some minor distraction. Yanique found it strange that there were no pictures on the wall.

Did they think a flower or something would make a patient want to keep the baby, she smirked questionably to herself?

The nurse handed her two pills, a mild sedation and a pain inhibitor along with a glass of water and instructed Yanique to swallow them. After about twenty minutes she felt soft cramps in her pelvic area. She lay there feeling tremendously alone.

Surely she couldn't have told her mother what she was doing. This fourth sorry ass man in her life who had impregnated her, did nothing more than give her the money for the procedure and told her to take care of it herself. She knew he wouldn't come around again.

Her mother's voice echoed in her head over and over again, *"Abortion is murder. It is an evil thing..."* She put her hands over her ears. Shut up! Shut up! Shut up! She thought she had screamed out loud, but realized no words had actually escaped her. She jumped slightly when the nurse tapped her on the shoulder and asked her if she was ready. The doctor walked in the door.

Chapter Two

The whooshing sound of the vacuum shattered Yanique's nerves as she lay there listening to the sound of a baby, her baby, being sucked out of her. As one small tear rolled down her cheek, she thought about the three daughters she had at home. She became peaked and started feeling very sick. Suddenly, without warning, she passed out.

After they managed to bring her back to consciousness, they informed her that everything had gone well. She was no longer pregnant. She sat in recovery with two other girls who seemed emotionally unattached to what they had also just done. They were just glad it was over with. When Yanique was well enough to be released, the nursing assistant called a cab for her to take her home. Shame overwhelmed her. It was the most traumatic experience of her life and the mere disgrace of it would never allow her to tell anyone. This was her secret to bear.

A deep depression consumed her and she lay in bed, unable to fully function. After two days of lying in bed, she felt a slight itching and stinging in her vaginal area. She couldn't shake it.

The intensity of the itching made her scratch until she had bleeding sores. She couldn't take it any longer and Yanique jumped in her car and stumbled into the nearest clinic. It was a free clinic, which enabled her to give a fake name. The entire time she was with the doctor, she held her head down.

Dr. Benoit was embarrassed for her as he identified the crab like creatures in her pubic area as lice. He saw her as a waif-like little girl in an adult body. For some reason he took note of the gray drabby sweater she had on. He felt sorry for her. He really wanted to reach out to help her. He sensed she was a lost soul.

She barely saw his face as he prescribed the cleansing shampoo and instructed her to clean all of her linens and disinfect her bed, chairs and other fabric furnishings the crab lice could live in. He suggested she shave all her pubic hair off. That was their first meeting, neither of them would ever remember it.

Ashamed, she drove to CVS Pharmacy and got some Rid. She had known what to use from when her daughters had issues at school with head lice. She didn't know if they were the same, but she did everything she could to disinfect their home. She never imagined she would have crabs in her pubic hair!

She pulled the strength together to get rid of the sea like blood sucking creatures. She was very thorough. When she finished with the extensive sterilizing, Yanique threw up several times. She couldn't describe the disgust she felt if she had to. She figured the only place she could have contracted crabs was at the abortion clinic. She hadn't been intimate in over two months. She wondered if they even cleaned the rooms between patients. Now she wondered if they even sterilized the equipment that was used on her. She would pray for her own salvation and hope that nothing else physical would result from this.

Feeling dizzy, her heart beat quickly as anxiety welled up inside her. She checked her daughters when they got home from school. She didn't know if crab lice spread to hair other than pubic hair. Her daughters were too young to have pubic hair. At least they were fine. Her mother had been at her sister's for over a week, so she wouldn't have been affected.

As the days passed, a grave sorrow surrounded Yanique. She could hardly function. No one really understood why. She barely spoke to people and her interaction with her family became scarce.

She tried forcing herself to go through the motions of being a loving mother to her children. Yanique found herself becoming increasingly paralyzed with fear, anxiety and depression. She started going out of the house less and less until one day, suddenly, without warning, sweat began pouring profusely from her pores. Her extremities were very cool to the touch, but she was extremely hot. Her heart raced rapidly. Her throat became very dry. She felt as if she couldn't breathe. As she took a quick gasp for air, her mind raced out of control.

"Am I having a heart attack? Am I going to die," she wondered panic stricken, still trying to catch her breath.

Noticing her mother's distress, her oldest daughter, Tayari, ran to her grandmother's room. "Nana Nadeige! Nana Nadeige! Something's wrong with mom. It's mom! It's mom! Please help!" she cried, banging on her grandma's door.

Nadeige quickly jumped out of the bed and ran to assist her daughter. Frightened at her daughter's appearance, Nadeige quickly called for an ambulance. Upon her arrival at Boston Medical Center, it was a quick determination that found Yanique was having a severe anxiety attack.

Dr. Benoit was on call that evening and was the treating physician for Yanique. While he was relatively sure of his originating diagnosis, he decided to err on the side of caution and requested a cardiogram which showed normal results.

Dr. Benoit told the assisting nurse to give Yanique a sedative. Once Yanique was in a stable, calm place, Dr. Benoit sat with her asking questions, trying to find out what excited her anxiety. She told him she didn't really know and that she had felt this increasing buildup of depression for weeks.

He felt a slight hint of familiarity with her for some reason, but couldn't quite place her. He recommended that she come to see him at his office at the Roxbury Community Comprehensive Health Center. He provided family health services including mental health care. She found him very calming and easy to talk to.

Yanique was a little on edge because she knew that Roxbury Comp was the free clinic she had gone to when she had the crabs. She didn't know if he was the same doctor and if it was did he recognize her. "Well, this time, I'll use my real name," she thought to herself.

Further chatter gave way to similarities in their lives. It turned out both she and the doctor were descendants of Haiti and they could both speak their native home language of French. Yanique felt comforted by their rooted connection.

"J'espère que vous vous sentez mieux... I hope you feel better," Dr. Benoit said with a smile as he handed her a prescription for depression. She smiled back at him as butterflies fluttered through her stomach.

Chapter Three

Dr. Charles Benoit grew up a native of Brooklyn, New York. Born on Sept 9, 1976, Charles had been an up and coming doctor of medicine since 2005. His affiliations included the Boston Medical Center as well as Roxbury Comprehensive Community Health Center. He always wanted to give back to his community.

He was a very handsome man who never took his looks for granted. He had chocolate brown skin, rounded eyes and could almost pass for a twin of Wyclef Jean. He was truly devoted to the art of medicine. He loved it. When he took the Hippocratic Oath, he proudly displayed the lines which meant the most to him by having it typeset and framed to display on his desk.

I will prescribe regimens for the good of my patients according to my ability and my judgment and never do harm to anyone.

I will give no deadly medicine to any one if asked, nor suggest any such counsel.

If I keep this oath faithfully, may I enjoy my life and practice my art, respected by all humanity and in all times; but if I swerve from it or violate it, may the reverse be my life.

Charles had met his wife Angela in medical school and together they decided he would be the one to covet the world of medicine while she became his wife as well as mother to his children.

Angela wasn't the slim, Barbie doll, trophy wife type one expects a doctor to have as a show piece. She was a tall, thick boned woman. Her skin was creamy brown in color. It was like a tea that was over creamed with a heavy creamer. Thick dark eyebrows shadowed over eyes begot with heavy droopy eyelids. Charles loved the sparkle in her eyes. He truly loved her. She made him laugh.

Angela could never understand how this ravishingly handsome man wanted to be with her. Knowing that he loved her was enough to give up her career and agree to be his wife.

By the time they were thirty-three, they had two kids and he had no more student loans. The City of Boston had paid off his loans after he signed an agreement to remain as a doctor in the Roxbury community for the next five years. A brand new Mercedes Benz lined the driveway of the home they purchased in Brookline, MA, a predominantly White suburban neighborhood.

Happiness was definitely two kinds of ice cream in this household and they felt truly blessed.

Chapter Four

Within ten days, Yanique showed up in Dr. Benoit's office. As with all of his patients Dr. Benoit was very professional. Yanique on the other hand immediately started flirting with him.

He recognized her flirtations but remained steadfast as a doctor. After one year of counseling, his assessment of her mental health was that of anxiety and depression, but after a year he still hadn't been able to determine the cause. She had also developed a mild case of agoraphobia which never seemed to hinder her ability to get to his office.

He treated her with medication and weekly counseling sessions. He found her sessions entertaining. They were never boring.

Sometimes he felt it was more of a help for her to just talk about whatever was on her mind. At times he shared some of his lifestyle with her. It was more like friends talking as friends.

Yanique routinely asked him out for a drink. She followed with telling him it would help with her agoraphobia. He often reminded her that she was his patient and nothing more. As time went on Yanique began taking her own little liberties by showing up in places she knew he would be. She wanted to see him at more than just the confines of the health center.

Dr. Benoit prided himself on being a man of God. He was a stellar man of the Haitian church community, holding fundraisers and sometimes hosting free clinics for those who couldn't afford to see a doctor.

He had been very active in progressing the Haitian ministries.

It was a rainy, thunderous Sunday morning as Charles stood on the podium in front of a large audience at the Jubilee Christian Center. Today he wanted to focus his sermon on the lack of faith in today's youths. As he reached the peak of his sermon, he looked over at his wife and was shaken to see Yanique sitting next to her, smiling and talking to his children.

The thunder roared loudly as he stuttered through his next lines. He continued to give surreptitious glances to see what was going on. The entire scene had thrown him off guard. Yet why should it have. He often invited his patients to church.

It bothered him when he saw Yanique. He himself didn't understand the pangs of guilt and foreboding that he felt at seeing Yanique with his family. He hastened his sermon and upon finishing sought out his family. Yanique had seen him coming and scurried out the door. He would, without hesitation, address this with her during their next session.

"Yanique, why are you showing up at my church?" Dr. Benoit asked, his voice clearly showing annoyance. He had to tread carefully. She was not only a patient, but a patient with psychotic issues.

"Dr. Benoit…" she stated, smiling coyly in mock disbelief, "You don't remember inviting me? You actually gave me a flyer to attend. I guess you thought I wouldn't come because of my fear of crowds, but I thought I would show you how much you are helping me get out of my shell and helping me with my anxiety. I didn't even know you saw me there. I sat next to these two adorable children. But after a while, I felt some anxiety setting in, so I left." Her tone was very matter-of-fact.

Dr. Benoit felt like an idiot who had overreacted. He couldn't have possibly assessed her to the degree that he could be wrong. He felt confused. How could that be? He shook the devil in his ear off his shoulder. He wasn't going to allow his confidence to be compromised. I'm not just a doctor, but I am one of the best. He was proud to see his treatment was actually working to the point where she could come out of the house for more than just their appointments.

As their sessions progressed, Yanique increased her request in asking Dr. Benoit out for a drink… "Just as friends, please, to show you my progress," she pushed. "I know you're married. I just feel like it would help me more."

He continued to maintain that it would not be a good idea. Her persistence was troublesome, but he did feel he was making some leeway in her recovery. He had yet to discover the core of what caused her anxiety.

Dr. Benoit began to see Yanique on numerous occasions outside of the clinic. He at first thought it was his imagination. He would spot her out of the corner of his eye, but then she would disappear when he would turn to say hello. Maybe his imagination was running in overdrive, after all, she did have issues with the agoraphobia. He had run into her at CVS, which appeared to be coincidental. And one evening while out at Chucky Cheese with his wife and children, she suddenly appeared with her three daughters. This time he surely knew it wasn't such a coincidence. He had noticed her following in her black sedan behind him. It appeared her anxiety was lessened, but this seemed out of line and surely out of character. "Was he overreacting?" he wondered. Turns out it was Yanique's youngest daughter's birthday and *he* seemed to be the one who was intruding. Whatever the circumstance, Charles was no longer comfortable with these flukes.

Chapter Five

Dr. Benoit sat across from the hospital administrator, April Washington, explaining the situation to her. His legs were crossed, glasses held in his hands, chewing the tips of them as he spoke, "I have a patient, Yanique LaCroix. I have been treating her for almost two years now for anxiety, depression and some agoraphobia. I'm also her primary care physician. I feel like she is stalking me. She seems to appear wherever I'm at these days. I even think she was sitting outside of my house. I find the situation delicate because of her mental anxiety. She's truly come a long way from when I first met her. She still needs treatment, but I would like to transfer her to another doctor. I feel this young lady has overstepped quite a few boundaries."

His hands were sweaty. This was the first patient he had ever asked to be transferred. He didn't want to believe he was actually buying in to his own paranoia." Charles handed Ms. Washington Yanique's case file.

April glanced through the file. One thing that stood out in her brief review was that Dr. Benoit had documented in her record that he had concerns for the safety of his family.

"If you really think it's that bad for you, perhaps we should relocate her to another clinic. Maybe send her over to Codman. They have a great mental health department," April suggested.

Charles gave the suggestion a fleeting thought, but quickly dismissed it. "I feel if we did that, it would undo all of the work we have accomplished so far. I don't think she needs to be removed from our facilities. Let's just reassign her to Dr. Balan. He seems pretty good."

"Okay, we'll do what you think is best," the administrator responded, "I will let you handle the details with Dr. Balan and you can tell the patient whatever you want."

April was a good business woman, but could care less about the patients. Hell, she barely cared about the doctors who she felt were all full of themselves. She referred to them all as pompous asses. Why did he even bother coming to me, she thought. Well, at least it's documented.

After consulting with Dr. Balan, who was more than willing to take over Yanique's care, Dr. Benoit anxiously awaited his next appointment with her.

He didn't want to tell her in the confines of such a sterile office environment. He also didn't want to bring on an anxiety attack. He had witnessed her anxiety attacks on a few occasions and they were harsh. He also didn't want her depression to go any deeper, let alone his being the cause of it. They were trying to lower her dosage of Lexapro. The Lexapro provided calmness to Yanique. This time when she innocently suggested they have dinner, he accepted. He was not surprised at her reaction to his acceptance. The transition should be smooth and not upsetting to Yanique.

Chapter Six

Small drops of blood spattered onto her thighs as a steady stream flowed into the sterilized cup Yanique held steadily beneath her vaginal opening. This was the main ingredient she needed for this fabulous dinner she was preparing for Dr. Benoit.

She had done everything in her natural power to get his attention and it hadn't worked. Yanique didn't typically buy into the voodoo religious views of her mother. But now that she was desperate, this was her last resort. She was running out of time.

Mother constantly said with her deep Haitian accent, "If you want to capture the man you love, put a little of your womanly flow in his food and make sure he eats it.

That's how I got your father and it was til death do us part."

Yanique was disgusted every time she heard that story. "Now I'm trusting in *your* God mother!" Yanique said out loud, eyes up to the sky to *her* God, as she crossed her fingers instead of saying a prayer.

She had to resort to other ways because finally Dr. Benoit had actually accepted her dinner invitation and his timing couldn't have been better. It was all she could do to get him to agree to come to her place to try one of her gourmet creations. She wasn't sure about his sudden change of heart. She had flirted with him for quite a while. She used all her womanly wiles that she could come up with. Apparently she wasn't very good at it, she thought, hell, three babies and no man, may be an indication. Maybe mother really knows best. Finally he was on his way, for whatever reason.

Yanique felt like a giddy high school girl as she set a small table. Fortunately, she had the house alone. Mother had taken her girls to Florida for the week of the annual Haitian festival. She had had two days to clean and start preparing.

Yanique actually was a great cook. Cooking helped to keep her calm and tonight she needed to stay composed. She liked to experiment with foods from other countries. She went out of her way to make what she learned was Dr. Benoit's favorite meal, a Tequila Marinated Chicken in a Mexican Molè Sauce.

The blood mixed very well in the molè sauce. It was undetectable and perhaps added a little extra spice. They would have dinner and she made a batch of authentic Hard Lemonade, going light on the tequila, adding a little honey to sweeten it just a bit. This definitely was not the manufactured Mike's Hard Lemonade. She would fill his glass with lots of ice. He's a doctor. After all, she wouldn't want him driving drunk.

The knock at the door startled her. She smoothed out her dress and opened the door welcoming him into her home.

"Good evening Charles," Yanique welcomed pleasantly, "Or should I refer to you as Dr. Benoit."

"Charles is fine," he responded. He seemed a little nervous. Dr. Benoit didn't want to jump right into the reason why he agreed to have dinner with her. He preferred a more public place, but felt dinner at her house would be harmless. He was very aware the crush she had harbored for some time, but he had to set the limitations.

The meal turned out to be very delicious. Charles was actually in awe of her cooking talents. What else was she hiding? She had never revealed this side. Small talk accompanied the dinner, as Yanique filled him in on how much she loved to cook. He had known her for over two years. She was his patient for family health services. He treated her for all of her issues, yet he was realizing that he hardly knew her. He was perplexed. Greedily, he ate his food, leaving nothing on his plate. With each fork he put in his mouth, Yanique grew more hopeful of the spell.

After a while she thought it was silly, silly and disgusting. But it was done now. He had eaten a full plate and even had seconds. He went very light on the Hard Lemonade being mindful of the reason he was there. And now it was time to discuss that reason with Yanique.

"Yanique you have crossed many boundaries with me and you know what they have been. I feel almost as if you have been stalking me. We haven't had any intimacies but I feel you could have fatal attraction tendencies. I have to transfer you as a patient to Dr. Balan. He's a good doctor and can provide you with the same care you have become accustomed to from me." He was very professional with his words.

Her hand started shaking. She dropped the glass that was in her hand. "What are you talking about? What boundaries have I crossed?" she asked, her voice quivering innocently. This isn't what she had expected. She took deep breaths to keep herself in control. She didn't want to embarrass herself with an anxiety attack in front of this man. Though her doctor he may be, she had fallen in love with him.

Dr. Benoit had anticipated an anxious reaction. He bent down to help pick up the large shattered pieces of glass. Yanique grabbed a hand towel, soaking up the remnants from the spill. A sudden urge to stab him with a piece of the glass ran through her mind. But just as quickly as the urge came, her body loosened and a smirk came over her face as her mother's words flowed through her.... *Just as a man partakes in the body of Christ, once he partakes the menstrual blood of a woman, he is destined to her.'* Her entire body language changed. She relaxed. She just had to believe

"Well, that's just fine, Charles." She said with sarcastic indifference. "If that is what you wish, set your boundaries."

She remained calm, wanting to hurry and rush him out the door. They drank a glass of wine and raised their glasses to each other. *Click.*

"To endings and to new beginnings," said Dr. Benoit with a sigh of relief.

"Yes, to new beginnings," she smiled pretentiously not letting out the anger that was welling up inside of her.

As she shut the door, tears dropped down her face. Signs of an attack were stifled as she vowed to believe in her mother's world of religious voodoo charm. She thought of how heartily he had eaten her food… had tasted her menstrual blood.

A wicked smile widened her lips across her face...." Gotcha! Yes Charles Benoit... I got you!"

Chapter Seven

Dr. Balan found Yanique to be a very troublesome patient. He was concerned about the obsession she festered for Dr. Benoit. Her depression was severe and he had to increase her medication. Though she tried hard to convince him otherwise, the change of doctors had emotionally affected her and the extremity of it frightened him and he felt it was best to give her in-patient treatment for at least a week.

Yanique was against this treatment but thought she should go along. She didn't want to be transferred completely out of RCCHC. She trained herself to be calm. She sat through a couple of group sessions and had daily individual counseling with the doctors at the Boston State Mental Institute. She thought of her three daughters and knew she should be there with them. If she was going to be a wilting flower, she wanted to be home. More importantly, she wanted to see Charles. Just as other patients rarely communicated with her, the nurses barely spoke to her either.

Yanique really couldn't take the solitude of the place so she had to play the game to get out of there. She knew how to do that, feign happiness and take the medication. Sometime the medication did help her. Other times she felt stifled by it, lethargic. After ten days, she was told she could go back to her outpatient treatment. She could resume her life. For her that meant she could resume her quest to capture the heart of Dr. Benoit.

Chapter Eight

It had been three months since Dr. Benoit had transferred Yanique's case to Dr. Balan. But it wasn't without its incidences. There were days when she showed up demanding Charles see her. Most times she would back down and leave the facility. A couple of times the police were called.

In order to get in to the clinic on days she didn't have appointments, Yanique had to resort to sexual antics with the security guards or the janitors. The rumors were spreading fast.

Dr. Benoit opened the door to exam room A. He had pulled the patient file out of the wall jacket but didn't look at the name. He had actually looked forward to this visit.

By some mishap when he found Yanique on his appointment schedule for a G-Y-N exam, he didn't bother to correct the problem. In fact, he decided to go ahead and do her exam.

Being short staffed there wasn't a nursing assistant in the room as is standard protocol. It was as if he lost his mind as soon as he saw her. His libido went completely out of control.

Yanique could tell by the way he looked at her that this was going to be more than just a simple G-Y-N exam. His eyes were glazed as if he was being controlled by a spell.....

She lay spread eagle, each foot gripped in the stirrups. Her ass hung over the tip of the table. She was nervous, her legs shaking a bit. Had she calculated this correctly? She was sure she had.

Charles had a gaping view of her vagina. Without a word, as if in a trance, he looked her directly in her eyes and instantly his body moved like deprivation of his senses was betraying his mind as he showed no resistance at all.

Having had seated himself in the doctors sliding stool, he lowered it and pulled himself so that his tongue went straight into her vagina. Yanique gasped relaxing her body as his warm tongue moved up and caressed her clitoris. He worked his tongue sensuously and quickly as her body moved like the rapture of a centipede until she almost shouted out in orgasm. One glance from Charles managed to make her remember where they were at.

"She's such a whore," he repeated in his mind, "She's so beautiful and headstrong". He was always psychoanalyzing things. It got old. He shut out the warning voice he heard in his head.

Charles stood up, grabbed Yanique's knees and rammed his penis deep into her pussy as he could and with only a few quick thrust he came hard. Clamping them together, he buried his face into her knees. After his penis returned to its flaccid normal state, he pulled out and fixed himself, questioning himself, "What the fuck did I just do?"

Yanique laid there, smiling, about to speak when the nurse assistant knocked and walked into the room. She sensed the discomfort as Dr. Benoit asked her to go get some additional slides so he could do the pelvic exam. She came back in quickly and handed him the slides. He had put on his rubber gloves and proceeded to do the exam. The assistant stayed in the room the remainder of the visit, much to Yanique's annoyance.

But the thrill she felt was satisfying. When he put his fingers in her with the gel on the rubber gloves, he snuck a finger up and rubbed her clit and it brought her to another orgasm. It took serious control to hold back her moans as she closed her eyes to take it in. She wanted that damn assistant out of the room.

It had taken three months, but Mama had said, "*Remain calm. Let the power of the spirit work through. Once he partakes of the wine from within you into his system, he will realize your worth. He will come crawling to you.*"

Yanique continued to trust in her mother's God.

Charles Benoit canceled the rest of his day and headed home. He had a wife he truly loved. He needed to spend some time with his family. He couldn't comprehend what had mysteriously come over him.

Yanique headed home drained, exhausted and feeling fulfilled. When she walked in the door she kissed her mother. She couldn't tell her what she had done, but she silently thanked her for her advice. Once she completely had what she wanted, she would fill her in.

Chapter Nine

Charles somehow lost his mind once this tryst started with Yanique. For the next year, Charles would beg her to meet him. They engaged in sexual relations at her home, at hotels, at the health center... even in the maintenance closets of the Boston Medical Center.

He had no control where Yanique was concerned. He couldn't stop himself. To make matters worse, Yanique's antics of showing up at the clinic unannounced demanding that he see her increased. She didn't care if he was with another patient or not. Since Dr. Benoit was trying to keep things hidden, he would try to cater to her as much as he could no matter how much it interfered with his other patients.

He thought back to a particular day Yanique showed up unannounced and he had to shove her into the closet at RCCHC to keep the medical director from seeing them together. He felt bad having to do that. He couldn't get through to her that their meetings needed to be more on the clandestine scale.

When it was safe for him to open the door, Yanique, instead of coming out yanked him inside. She had been dressed in a short miniskirt and she seldom wore panties because she always wanted to be ready for him. Yanique was very agile. She had grabbed onto a low hanging rod. It was a strong rod. She ordered him to lower his pants. His adrenaline was on fire at the fear of someone opening the door. Once again, however, he couldn't stop himself. He did as she instructed. She swung her legs around his hips and lowered herself onto his upright hard cock. She lifted herself up and down controlling the rhythm of the thrusts until they both came. It wasn't until then when the smell of sex, permeated with the scent of dirty mops and chemical cleaning supplies, had they truly realized where they were. He pulled up his pants and straightened himself out so that he again looked like a respectable physician. He suggested she wait a few moments before walking out and to make sure no one was in the hallway. He walked out unseen by any of the staff.

Two of Benoit's colleagues figured out what was going on and tried to talk to him men to man. He brushed their admonishing aside and told them he knew what he was doing and to mind their own business. The only place Yanique wasn't showing up at was his home. That made him confident he had her handled. In fact, she was essentially handling him. She would sometimes bring him lunch. Although Charles looked forward to her meals, some days he didn't have time to eat. She was often refreshing her *ingredients* to make sure her incantations wouldn't wear off. She didn't know if she had to update it from time to time.

"She just needs to get it out of her system. It will pass," he expressed to his colleagues. They were not convinced, "No Doc. You need to get her out of your system. What the hell did this girl do to you? You better watch out. You may have a Jodi Arias on your hands!"

His cockiness wouldn't allow him to consider such a thing. "Man, I have been providing psychoanalysis for this girl for three years. She's not built like that."

But the intensity of the relationship was starting to slow Charles down. He couldn't keep up this façade much longer. He wanted to put it to bed. He knew it had to be done delicately. Whatever hold she had on him was beginning to wane. His life was going in a different direction. His career was blossoming, in spite of being with her. There were just too many close calls. He finally decided he wanted out. The hold Yanique had was loosening. He couldn't wrap his head around his own loss of sanity. This was a blatant disrespect to his wife, but he couldn't control himself.

It was time to let go of this bad baggage. He would do it slowly so as not to make her any more crazy than she already was. She had her normal moments but there were days where she actually seemed schizophrenic. Had he diagnosed her correctly? His arrogance was diminishing.

Chapter Ten

Yanique had planned a nice romantic evening with Charles. She had cooked him another fantastic meal. He seldom came to her house. She was getting a little tired of these clandestine meetings. But tonight they would be celebrating.

Often Charles would buy her nice fancy clothes, beautiful jewelry and the likes. She decided to put on a yellow, fitting sundress he gave her that matched the yellow sunflowers she put on the table. They had been fanatically dating for over a year. He couldn't get enough of her. The thought made her squeal out loud and she couldn't wait to hear his knock on the door.

Charles arrived a little late due to an emergency at Boston Medical Center. Yanique didn't mind this time. She knew he would be there. When he finally arrived, Yanique didn't notice the look of disdain he had given her. Tonight the sight of her was making him sick. She figured he was tired, but she would make him happy as she always did.

Charles noticed how joyful she was and figured he would make sure this closing evening would be a nice one for her. He would start weaning her off of him or should that be himself off of her. What had happened to the logical Charles seemed to be wearing off. It was almost as if he had looked in the mirror and said Candy Man five times. He had to chuckle at himself for that one.

As they sat eating, Yanique seemed anxious and he wondered if she had taken her medication. What was going on with her? "Baby guess what?" Yanique asked Charles teasingly and in a baby voice.

"What?"

He tried not to express his sheer irritation. She got up and walked around the table to his side of the table. She took his hand and touched it to her belly. He was instantly repulsed as she stood there squealing like a banshee.

"I'm pregnant!" She pulled out the pregnancy test and showed him the results. She happily clapped her hands like a child. The sirens in his head were loud and menacing. This was beyond concrete evidence of his affair. This would destroy his marriage. He still loved his wife. He still couldn't fathom his weakness with this psychotic patient.

Charles put his elbows on the table, hands fisted together upon his forehead. He was shaking his head in disbelief. He had woven the web just a little tighter and was putting a noose around his own neck. He never bothered to use a condom. He had known her medical history. He never gave birth control a thought. He made stupid assumptions.

Charles thought hard and long before he spoke, "Yanique, you have to terminate this pregnancy. You already have three kids. I have two. I do not want to leave my wife and children. So why don't you let me take care of this? I will take you for an abortion. I will be there to hold your hand. If it's easier for you, I will do it myself." His voice was calm yet panicked. A pregnancy would reveal his shame. She was an Achilles heel for him at this point. He needed to get his life back.

Charles saw all the signs of an impending anxiety attack. A full blown anxiety attack would simply add fuel to the fire. He didn't need this right now, he said, annoyed, "Yanique, breathe….use the techniques I taught you…"One," he said steadily, two, three… by the time he got to ten, she was breathing normally.

For Yanique, this was the ultimate blow. She thought this past year had brought them closer together. This act of selfishness took her for a loop. She thought of the other men that had been in her life. She couldn't believe this was happening. Her head was spinning. She paced back and forth in her living room then started throwing up. He had never seen this side of her. More missed symptoms he surmised heartlessly. Oh well, that's Dr. Balan's problem now.

Chapter Eleven

Yanique fell to the ground in a fetal position. She stuck her thumb in her mouth and started rocking herself back and forth. Charles just didn't care. He simply got up and walked out the door, leaving Yanique to her own psychosis. At best he hoped she would choke on her own vomit.

An ambulance came careening around the corner. Nadeige had come home and found Yanique in a semi-catatonic state. She called Dr. Balan who immediately instructed her to call an ambulance and have them take her to the state mental institution. He would meet them there he told her as he grabbed his keys and headed towards his car. He knew this relationship with Dr. Benoit would cause trouble. Why hadn't he reported him to the medical disciplinarian board himself?

Upon arriving at the state institution, Dr. Balan was completely surprised at what he found. Yanique was her normal self and insisting that no one give her any medication.

Under the guidelines of patient/doctor confidentiality, Yanique told Dr. Balan she was pregnant. "Charles was a little upset and suggested I have an abortion. But Dr. Balan, as you know and something Charles had never been able to figure out, the abortion I had was what triggered my first anxiety attack. I now can hardly believe that the love of my life just suggested I have an abortion."

Dr. Balan cringed at the personalization of her calling Dr. Benoit by his first name. He was at a loss. How did he get tangled in this web? "How did you get Dr. Benoit to have sex with you Yanique?"

"Well, my mother's religion hinders on the voodoo beliefs from Haiti. She gave me a trick to try. I constantly fed him my menstrual blood in the food I cooked for him. Whenever, I had a period, I would fill tubes of the blood and keep them frozen and would use them to cook in his dinners. I'm a fantastic cook Dr. Balan, did you know that? The funny thing is, now that I am pregnant, I won't be able to serve him any additional. I don't know how it works. I hope it doesn't wear off so fast." Her voice was childlike and innocent.

Dr. Balan was sickened by what he was hearing. He has a psychologically ill patient, now pregnant by a colleague of his. He had to call Dr. Benoit to get him to handle this a little more delicately. He suggested a patient consult conference. Immediately.

Chapter Twelve

"Dr. Benoit, I am fully aware of what's going on between you and Yanique. I just don't know what to do about it. Clearly, what you were never able to diagnose was what caused her anxiety attacks in the first place.

This poor young woman had an abortion that completely affected her psychological makeup. She's borderline bipolar. Now here you are making the same suggestion of abortion. And on top of that, she fell into a semi-catatonic state and you left her there like that. What the hell is wrong with you?" By the end of this conversation he was yelling almost at the top of his lungs.

Dr. Benoit was thrown off at the directness of Dr. Balan. He had always considered Balan a wimp. He stood up, slammed his hands down on the desk and yelled back, "You stay out of my *Goddamn* business!"

"She is *my* Goddamn patient thanks to you asshole! Apparently you didn't realize how good of a doctor I really am. Imagine, someone better than you." Dr. Balan's anger was rising to the point of wanting to incite physical violence. "You treated her for three years! Had you known much about her, perhaps you wouldn't be digesting her menstrual blood."

Dr. Benoit was taken aback. Bile filled his throat. "What the fuck are you talking about?" he asked, his voice shaking as the words came stuttering through.

"Yes," said Dr. Balan, his wrath not subsiding. "The girl put her menstrual blood in the food she was feeding you. Don't you know her Haitian religious background? Her roots? Your damn roots? You didn't consider any of that? With how you have responded, it seems to have worked! Maybe you should consider adding that treatment to your practice. Do what you have to do Dr. Benoit and try to remember that oath you took. You seem to have forgotten the words. I suggest you find a solution other than abortion."

Charles was silent as he walked towards the door, his head held low.

"Oh, by the way, in case you care, Yanique is fine. She will be released this afternoon to the care of her mother," he informed him. "She really is glowing," Dr. Balan added sarcastically. His annoyance at being dragged into this mess had reached an all-time high.

Charles walked out of the office. He didn't know what direction to go in. He would find some kind of way for that baby not to be born.

Chapter Thirteen

Once again, Yanique was released from the state mental institution and free to go about her day to day. She didn't have another appointment with Dr. Balan for two days. She felt good. She was having another baby. This one was special. His daddy is a doctor! At the very least, he would be financially cared for, unlike the other three children.

She was hoping for a boy. She already had three daughters. As she sat there daydreaming about a life with Charles her cell phone rang and much to her surprise it was him. He spoke to her as if nothing had happened, "Hey babes, I'm free for the afternoon. I am coming to get you for lunch. Are you free? Will your mother watch the girls?"

"Of course," Yanique said, her heart beating with excitement. "Do you mind if we stop and pick up my prescriptions first? My Ob/Gyn called in some medications for me and Dr. Balan approved."

"Sure," he said, his voice cautious. He had called in a prescription for her as well. This was moving along just fine.

Yanique never really paid attention to her medications. She simply did as she was told. She had three healthy babies already and knew what she needed to do to sustain this pregnancy. Dr. Balan had said he would have to adjust her psych medications. She had already decided to stop taking them.

As she went to check-out, the pharmacy clerk told her the pharmacist would like to speak to her to go over her medications. The pharmacist was confused.

"Yanique, this medication here prescribed by Dr. Charles Benoit is called Misoprostol. If you take those, you will miscarry the fetus within three days. The other prescription, from Dr. Meekes is a prescription for prenatal vitamins. So I am a little confused. I imagine you are a bit undecided? If so, instead of these pills, perhaps you may consider other alternatives. The misoprostol will cause major cramps until you extract the fetus out into the toilet. It will come out in pieces and at various times. So perhaps some other alternative would be best."

Anger welled up inside her. How dare Charles call in a prescription for her to make her baby abort itself. Did this pharmacist just tell her it would come out in pieces? Yanique started doing the techniques she had learned in order to halt the oncoming anxiety attack she felt.

She ran back to the car and yanked open the door.

"What the fuck is wrong with you Charles Benoit?" She threw the bottle in his face hitting him in the corner of his right eye. He flinched.

"You do not need to have this baby Yanique!" Teeth clenched, he was bordering on rage at having been hit as well as the situation of the pregnancy.

"Get it together Charles. Get it together Charles," he told himself silently as he touched his finger to his mouth to wet it with spit to put on the slight cut he felt at the corner of his eye. She stood outside of the black Mercedes Benz, doing her calming exercises for five minutes.

"Get in Yanique," he ordered.

Yanique got in the car refusing to say anything else. Her feelings were clearly hurt. But she felt she had the upper hand. He would come around eventually. Hell, he didn't really have a choice.

He drove to her favorite restaurant. It was an outdoor spot and it was a beautiful June night. The meal was initially met with silence. As their evening progressed, she noticed a mellow change in his demeanor. She wanted wine, but good mothering starts in the womb she told herself. Yanique felt this pregnancy was her redemption to the abortion that had spiraled her soul into many spinning cycles.

But what she hadn't noticed was after throwing the prescription at him, he took the pills out of the bottle and put them in his pocket. And what she didn't realize at that moment, remnants of those pills were floating in the water she was drinking.

Charles picked up his glass of water and held it up to her as if in defeat of the idea of the abortion. "Well," he said, "I guess, here's to us and our unborn." He clicked his glass against hers. She smiled and again thought, *'til death do us part…thanks mom!'*

Charles took her out three times that week. He even spoke of leaving his wife. Yanique had no guard up against anything he was saying or doing. She figured the menstrual blood she had given him on several occasions was in full effect.

Chapter Fourteen

It was an early Sunday morning as Yanique danced around her room singing I Feel Pretty, from Westside story, until all of a sudden she felt a tremendous painful cramp that brought her to her knees. She screamed for her mother.

They drove to Carney Hospital. She was given a blood pregnancy test which showed positive. They then did a pelvic ultrasound, but no pregnancy was seen. The nurse practitioner at Carney suggested that perhaps she was having a miscarriage.

"No," she argued, "there is no bleeding. How could that be? Maybe it is just too soon for you to see it on the ultrasound." She chose to ignore their diagnosis. The cramps had calmed down. She convinced herself that all was good. She went back home.

Yanique continued to ignore any of the symptoms that could possibly indicate she was having a miscarriage. But two days later, the pain became too unbearable. She called Charles.

The wailing scream of her voice was like that which emulated a rabbit getting eaten by a coyote. He felt slight pangs of guilt, but all he could think of was it would be over soon and she would be none the wiser that he had been dosing her drinks with the Misoprotol.

It was a slow evening at the hospital so it was easy for him to leave his position and go pick her up. He took her to Beth Israel Hospital because it was a hospital he wasn't affiliated with. Not many, if anyone, would recognize him there.

After another positive blood test, the doctors at Beth Israel followed the same procedures by doing an ultrasound. They too were unable to see a viable pregnancy, but what they did see was an ectopic pregnancy. The fetus was growing in the tube and the pregnancy would have to be terminated or it would rupture the tube and could possibly kill her.

Tears smudged the make-up down her face. She grabbed the attending physician and got on her hands and knees as she begged him in front of Charles, to make this a viable pregnancy. "Please!" She cried, begging, "please save my baby!" Charles could barely look at her. All he could think was, "If only I had waited, this pregnancy would have terminated itself." His stupidity and risk he had taken with his medical license by writing the prescription was apparent. But he would tell her they could get her pregnant again… that would buy him some time.

The physician recommended they give her an injection of Methotrexnite to treat the ectopic pregnancy. She asked Charles for his medical opinion and he advised her to take it.

"Yes, Yanique, I agree with the doctors here. It's not a viable pregnancy. It's in your tubes not in your uterus. There is nothing that can be done." He sounded forlorn and very sad. In his mind, he was doing the cabbage patch dance.

Worn down and leery, Yanique consented to the injection. Her mental state was waning. Another baby being flushed away. She cursed this voodoo God her mother had made her believe in. She cursed life itself. Throughout the tears and her hysteria, she heard Charles whispering to the physician about the misoprostol. At least she thought she did. No, she was sure.

"Combining the shot with the fact that she was taking Misoprostol, should make the pregnancy terminate easier. But it appears she has some rupturing and we have to do an emergency laparoscopy and remove the ectopic tissue and her fallopian tube."

All this medical talk was becoming unbearable. Yanique had signed the consent forms with the comfort of Dr. Benoit. Mentally, she checked out. When she came to she was in a hospital room hooked up to the necessary equipment with Charles asleep in the chair next to her.

Hate and rage began welling up inside her. She thought she was yelling, but when she called Charles' name it was soft and whispery. It was low, but it startled him.

While he had spent many nights in hospital beds for quick naps, and uh yes, quickies, his back ached from the discomfort of the position he had slept in.

"Charles what did you do with the prescription bottle of the drug you tried to get me to take to miscarry?"

"Oh, I threw those away when you threw it at me and said you would never take it honey." His response was slow and calculated. She knew he was lying. She thought back to the constant dinners he suddenly started taking her to as if they were going to become one big happy family. The juice he had her drinking and all the new found care. She should have seen it.

Finding her voice she asked, "I heard you tell that doctor that I was taking that drug! I never took that drug, why would you tell him that!?" Yanique's hesitation was momentous. "Oh my God... Oh my God..." she yelled, "YOU KILLED MY BABY! YOU KILLED MY BABY" Yanique was screaming at the top of her lungs.

The dam of rage had broken wide open. She jumped out of the bed and was instantly upon him with her hands around his neck trying to choke him.

It took three orderlies to get her off of him and get her sedated.

"Call Dr. Balan over at RCCHC. He is treating her for her Mental Health Issues."

Charles suggested after catching his breath. Once again, he had not anticipated her reaction.

Chapter Fifteen

It took two weeks to get Yanique back to a somewhat normal state.

It took one day after for her to contact a lawyer and the medical board to start an immediate investigation of Dr. Charles Benoit's medical treatment for his patients. Dr. Balan would be her supporting witness.

The staff was notified immediately that Dr. Benoit was to have no prescription privileges and then within a week, they were informed that he would no longer be seen around the hospital. The staff was not without knowledge of what was going on. The gossip about his relationship with Yanique had been widespread. Even other patients were talking about it.

The FBI interviewed every single nurse or affiliate who had anything to do with Dr. Benoit.

By the following January, 2013, Dr. Benoit was no longer a doctor. All of his licenses had been revoked and he was under investigation by the DEA.

It was clear that he was practicing medicine fraudulently when he wrote Yanique the prescription for Misoprostol. His competence was also questioned when he engaged in a sexual relationship with a mentally ill patient. It was very clear that he lacked good moral character which undermines the public confidence in the integrity of the profession.

After a year of being in and out of mental facilities, and several failed suicide attempts by Yanique, a lawsuit was brought against Charles Benoit and Roxbury Comprehensive Community Health Center. Yanique was awarded a three million dollar settlement.

The conclusions were that Dr. Benoit engaged in the practice of medicine fraudulently with gross misconduct also with the capacity to deceive or defraud. He lacked good moral character engaging in conduct that undermined the public confidence in the integrity of the medical profession.

He had held no honor for those infamous words displayed on his desk from the Hippocratic Oath.

All were astonished. But you see, further investigation would find sealed documents that were released during the trial.

There was no Charles Benoit. There was Daniel Beaumond.

At the age of seventeen, Daniel Beaumond, was diagnosed with multiple personalities. He had gone through several integration methods and the dominant personality, Andrew, was able to convince the others to 'play dead' for a while and let Charles take over. But even though they were enjoying the niceties of life, it was a struggle to live such clean cut lives all of the time.

They felt Charles Benoit was getting too much of the attention, living too much of their lives. They were tired of the same ole Angela. And this Yanique... well she had been more to their liking.

Charles Benoit peered out of the window as security lamps illuminated the grounds of the Massachusetts State Mental Institution with pale, yellowing light. His body was silhouetted in an eerie glow. Crumbling mortar and missing bricks made up the buildings in his outer view. He was up on the third floor ward. He felt the need to remain in silence out of reverence for his past eight years of life.

It had been easy for him to falsify the documents of having gone to medical school. Oh, he had gone for a while. He had acquired the student loans, but he fully never completed any classes. Yet his debt increased as he registered and took several classes not pertaining to medicine. Once he met and fell in love with Angela, he knew he had to get her out of the school. She would be none the wiser. She would be the doctor's wife at home to go along with his façade. So he thought why not marry her and leave her home with some kids. It would be the perfect life picture. And hell, he thought, perhaps he may actually save some lives.

This evening, as with every evening now, Charles Benoit stood looking out that window from his room on the fourth floor and listened. He was in Room 48. There were twenty-four rooms on his ward. Each door contained two locks... two *clicks* per room. Every evening as the night's silence rolled in, because of his extraordinary hearing, he could hear each click of every lock as each patient's chamber was locked. Each night he would count down, *click, click, click* ... til they reached his door count at forty-eight clicks!

Charles Benoit, once an in-house resident doctor, now a lifetime resident of the State Mental Institution of Massachusetts.

Every day Yanique drove by the institution, now in her new Black BMW Series 7, wickedly smiling. "Got you Dr. Benoit. I got your ass!"

Click...

My best orgasm was with a guy who was psychotic. There was nothing he did that was particularly special, but it was the intensity of his psychotic energy that made it so erotic."There's something about the energy of a crazy person" — Alexandra'

48 CLICKS

Sharing Secrets

Chapter One

Charlene Abbott laughingly licked her lips as she put on some fresh lip gloss. With a wicked smile, she mosied on back to the living room where she was having a bachelorette pajama party with her girlfriends.

She was the center of attention as the self-proclaimed sex counselor. "Hmm, maybe I should make that the orgasm machine," she smiled at herself in the mirror. "Well, I am sure there are others, who have accomplished this, but how many can truly say they had forty-eight orgasms in forty hours!"

This new girl standing in the mirror was a far cry from the girl who at twenty-eight got naked in front of her faux mama, Ms. Tina, and asked her to show her where her clitoris was. Ms. Tina had no other choice but to oblige.

Ever since Charlene first had sex at the age of eighteen, she had wondered what an orgasm felt like. She laughed at the thought of her first time. Hell, the dry humping had felt better than that. She had even picked up the telephone and called, Kevin, her first. She still had a vivid memory of him. He was actually Gay now. She wondered if that was her fault.

"Hey Kevin, we have to try this again", she had demanded, "It didn't feel like anything". After their tenth time together, out of sheer frustration, she headed to the gynecologist.

"I think something is wrong with me. I think I'm frigid or something. Once my boyfriend puts it in me, it doesn't feel like anything."

The doctor damn near fell out of her chair and had to control herself from laughter. Never had a patient come into her office and revealed that, especially, a teenager.

In keeping within her trained professionalism, Dr. Simone's first response was, "Before we get into that, are you on birth control? Let's worry about unplanned pregnancy first." She didn't want another teenage pregnancy to occur and if she could put a stop to one, she was happy to do so.

After confirming the birth control issues, Dr. Simone told her, "Just make sure the young man is stimulating your clitoris more and giving you foreplay. That's the best I can give you."

After all, Dr. Simone, although a gynecologist who knew the anatomy of a woman, she, herself, wasn't too experienced in the sex department. Hell, she wasn't even willing to go 'downtown'.

Charlene left the doctor's office without answers. She had heard of the clitoris, but didn't really know where it was on her body. Was this what sex really felt like with a penis entering her...."NOTHING!" Yet, all things leading up to that felt pretty good.

After reading all those romance novels where these women describe their incredible orgasms, Charlene realized, there definitely had to be more to it than this dissatisfaction!

She often listened to Ms. Tina and some of her girlfriends talk constantly about the orgasms they had with their men, or women for that matter. Charlene desperately wanted to step outside of her current boundaries.

At thirty-eight, after two husbands and one remarkable daughter, Charlene met a wonderful guy named Nick. He was everything a girl could want in a man. He was somewhat good looking. He worked hard. He treated her daughter with respect. He cooked their meals and basically treated Charlene as the princess she felt she was. He often said that he wanted to be a farmer and live a country lifestyle.

Sadly, in spite of all that, he never wanted intimacy. She began to feel she was the problem. Maybe she was too fat. She went to the gym and started working out. She lost twenty pounds. She went blond and added warm highlights. She flirted with him. She wore sexy lingerie. She even tried waking him up with blow jobs.

Absolutely nothing was gained. Their entire lives were a regime of lackluster. She still couldn't move herself to leave him. Everything else was perfect. But after two years complete with no intimacy she was compelled to seek out James.

Charlene had met James in high school and they had reconnected on Facebook a few years back. James immediately started in about how hot she had been back then, but thought he never had a chance. He totally boosted her ego.

After a month of illicit Facebook banter, he showed up in Las Vegas. His schedule was hectic and rushed, but they managed to have dinner and a drink as the sparks flew between them. James, however, was married and lived in Nebraska. He was a chronic cheater with an insatiable libido and a wife who couldn't keep up with him. He invited Charlene to Nebraska.

Charlene told Nick she was going to visit her girlfriend in Colorado. Her nerves were in shambles. She had never done anything like this before and she didn't want to get caught. She took a flight to Colorado. When she got off the plane, she sent Nick a text so it would show her location as Colorado. She always made sure she had her GPS tracking on. Once confirming to Nick that she was in Colorado she boarded a small plane to Nebraska where one thing led to another and BAM! *48 freaking clicks.*

For four straight days she indulged in unadulterated sex. Her body had never been in so many twisted positions. She had never been fulfilled so much in her life. This made up for all she was missing out on with Nick. Where else could she go from here?

It had been her one affair. She wanted to live honestly and wasn't ready to give up the material world that engulfed her. Nick had made her lose her self-confidence. James helped her begin to find it again.

Her orgasms had been so powerful that before her wedding, and of course, after having had forty eight freaking orgasms in forty hours of those four days with James, Charlene wanted to brag about it to her closest friends. After this she vowed to never bring it up again, nor cheat on her husband to be.

Her mind flashed back…. *Click! Click! Click!* She hadn't thought to actually keep track of her orgasms until after the fifth one when she noticed a counter in the back of James' truck. The visuals were as vivid as if it was yesterday.

Without hesitation upon arriving at a secluded destination in the woods, with one big hand placed on the small of her back, James pinned her in place over the hood of the small recreational vehicle Polaris Razor. He drove his penis deep in and out of her as the vehicle moved rhythmically with their movements, back and forth with every sharp thrust. Their bodies were hot and sweaty as the hot sun beat down upon them. They were loud and his thrusts were violent. She was free and abandoning all chains that were binding her. As she lay, her back burning on the Razor, she felt every inch of him. James wrapped his fingers through her long blonde highlighted hair.

He pulled her head back and looked into her eyes as she gave way to her first orgasm of the morning. Her first explosion was strong, but not fully volcanic. It was amazing. Her moans and cries grew louder, but before she could explode again, James flipped her over effortlessly and continued pumping into her with enough force to make her teeth chatter. This was no gentle lovemaking. This was passionate, vengeance sex, long overdue from her ho-hum existence with her fiancé and she loved every single minute of it.

She snapped out of her conscious trance and remembered she had a house full of women drinking alcohol and ready to share their most erotic orgasms. She was sure none could top hers.

Charlene sashayed back into the living room in her sexy lingerie which was a requirement for everyone to wear. She wanted everyone to be as transparent as possible because lots will be revealed as they played the Vagina Diaries Truth or Dare.

It would be a great night of intimate sharing. She knew these girls had nothing on her, after all she will be quick to remind them, she is the orgasm queen, the *O.Q.*, as Theresa had called her. There can only be one queen. Perhaps one can follow up as the princess she laughed to herself. Let's see what they come up with.

Chapter Two

Victoria sat in disbelief at what she was hearing coming out of these women's mouths. She never believed women actually sat around directly talking like this. She had never been this open with her friends.

Victoria Smith was one of three blonds in the room. She hadn't been in a relationship in over six years. Basically at this point she had given up.

She was the CEO of her own permanent makeup school, Victoria's Permanent Makeup. She was a self-made millionaire. She traveled the world by way of Australia, London, Paris and the likes, but she was still alone. Love just didn't seem to be on her horizon.

Beauty was her business. She found herself caught up in not only her clients' appearances, but also her own as well. She worked out excessively. She dieted excessively.

But the elements of aging worked against her. It was all futile. The weight wouldn't come off, her muscles remained flabby no matter how much she worked out. She wore an abundance of makeup to look younger, yet sometimes she could hear the snickers of her younger clients. Even though they snickered, they were still impressed with her work and always came back.

The sexual part of all her relationships had been epic failures. She had been married for ten years and had raised two daughters. She only knew two of the girls in this group, the host and Theresa.

Theresa had mentioned her oral explorations to her at one point and Victoria was appalled and swiftly shut the conversation down. Now here she was amongst these women who seem to be relishing in the idea of sharing this information.

Victoria's last relationship with Michael was filled with anxiety and trepidation. She never had allowed herself to trust him completely. They had clicked together well. They enjoyed similar things. She marveled at his diligence of becoming a firefighter. It had taken him over four years and she continually encouraged him. He sure had the body.

When she discovered he was watching porn movies, he invited her to join him. She expected him to be apologetic. She was devastated. She felt it was as if he had cheated so she ended the relationship.

"Was I truly that much of a prude?" Maybe she had to make some changes so she could enjoy sex. She was sure going to listen to what these gals were putting out. Maybe she could get Michael back. She never stopped loving him. She was afraid to get deeper involved so perhaps she was just looking for excuses. What if their sex life became fabulous? Would she have been stuck with him?' She pondered all of her thoughts.

A glass of wine was definitely in order. Hmmm, maybe something a little stronger. Perhaps some tequila. She grabbed a shot, swigged it down and then took a glass of wine and sat on the floor. She would listen. She would relax. Maybe find a new side of herself. Wait, was she getting horny? A giggle escaped her lips. She was excited to hear more.

Irene sat gingerly eyeing Charlene. "Orgasm Queen, " she mimicked sarcastically and silently to herself. She may have had forty-eight orgasms in a forty hour period, yes an amazing feat, but how many has she had in her life.

Irene was sixty years old, but her age was undetectable. The average person would have felt she was fifty at best. She had had her fair share of men with countless orgasms. Her viewpoint, one she tried to instill in her close girlfriends was, *if you make love to a man, you make love to every part of him.* Nothing was off limits.

As she looked Charlene up and down, she wondered what made her so lucky. She had a great side piece in James, who was capable of sustaining an erection for hours on end according to Charlene. I wonder if he had some Cialis. Now she was about to marry a respectable guy. He had money, he had his health and he could give her every materialistic thing she wanted. Charlene was a sexy little thing too. I'll give her that. But damn, why can't I find a man?' She mused. 'I'm a good woman.'

Probably every single woman in that room was wondering the same thing.

"Irene, Irene!" yelled Charlene. Irene hadn't noticed Charlene pulled her name out of the bowl to be next to share. "Are you distracted? It's your turn. Care to share your best orgasm with us or do you have a dare instead?"

Irene had already wandered into her sexual zone. This was her forte. Let the sharing begin. "For now," she said sneakily, "I have a truth and one that I think you will enjoy!"

"Well, I was messing around with this guy named Warren. We were always open to trying new things. He was a freckled face guy, not so great looking, but looks have never really mattered to me.

We started out with some long sensual kissing and our normal foreplay as he got my pussy really wet. I don't think I need to describe foreplay, but let me know if I do." She hesitated to see if anyone needed guidance. Kathy had wanted to ask for some suggestions, but it was futile because she wouldn't try it anyway.

"Okay, I got some lubricant and rub it around my anus. I didn't let it get to a sloppy point. Vaseline worked fine. Just use a little because it is kind of thick. Warren had a medium sized dick, but it had an enormous head on it. I had to make sure he

would move slowly and carefully. I was pretty agile back then. I laid on my back in a half sit up position with my ass hanging off the edge of the bed. He was standing at the edge. I had a high bed. I took one hand and reached up and grabbed his penis and guided just the huge head of his dick right on the inner/outer edge of my ass. Maybe I should just say the beginning of the opening. You know how when a guy misses the vagina and goes into the ass instead. Well, like that.

The intensity of the feeling was indescribable! As he continued stroking my ass with the head of his penis, begging to put his whole dick in, he put two fingers into my vagina and moved them in and out really fast which is why I said be very wet."

Small beads of sweat started forming on the top of her forehead. Her eyes closed as if she was feeling what she was expressing. She wanted to throw her head back. Victoria, upon noticing Irene's nipples were shooting straight out, handed her a cold glass of wine, smiled and sat back down and began fanning herself.

Irene continued.

"That combination brought me to an extreme orgasm. I mean extreme! I was trembling. I was speechless. I balled up into a fetal position. Warren asked if I was okay. I said absolutely nothing. I actually couldn't respond. The intensity of it had literally scared me to death. It scared me so badly, I asked him to leave.

Around midnight he came back banging on the door drunk and belligerent. He had felt used. I let him in because he was making such a ruckus and I didn't want him to upset or wake the neighbors.

I opened the door, Warren swiftly, unexpectedly grabbed me and bent my arm back and pushed me down on the bed and raped me so hard I threw up at the pain of it. After he finished, I got up. I left my own apartment and told him, by the time I get back, you better be gone."

Tears streamed down her face. The room was silent with the exception of light sobs from a couple of the other guests. Irene had relived the intensity of the orgasm, almost ashamed that it had been the best one she ever had as she then revealed having had been raped.

She hadn't shared that story with anyone before. When she got back, he had gone and as she wished she never heard from him again. It was thirty years ago and the enormity of it had just hit her.

"Sorry ladies, I didn't mean to go there. Let me just get myself refreshed." The momentum of the party had changed.

She walked off into the bathroom to regroup. She came back to a line of women who took turns giving her a hug and show of their support.

Irene looked humbled, her emotions blushing. She wasn't used to this kind of emotional display, but she willingly accepted each hug.

"Wow… I didn't mean to take it there. I appreciate your concern. I'm fine. I'm okay. I guess that had been weighing on me for a while. But hey, it's a party. Let's move back onto the orgasms!!! Come on O.Q. Why don't you tell us a few of your forty-eight?"

The girls laughed with her. It had been an unexpected turn. Charlene had felt bad for Irene, but she didn't particularly like her so she didn't care. She was introduced to her by Theresa, so she tolerated her. Actually, they simply tolerated each other.

"Yes, Charlene, *O.Q.!* Orgasm Queen, let's hear about a few of your forty-eight," the girls chimed. "Yes!" one of the girls cried out, "By the way, mind if I go to my bag and get out some of my sex toys? Maybe a dildo or two!" They all laughed.

Chapter Three

"Okay ladies," the queen bee said, gulping down her fourth Bud light. Her face reddened. She was slightly uncomfortable. She had never been this candid, but she truly wanted to share this. She wanted other women to enjoy these incredible sensations.

"James leaned me back and grabbed BOTH of my knees and pressed my thighs apart. I was WIDE open completely to his gaze. You know what I mean? For a moment I was embarrassed. I fought to close my legs, but his hands were like a vice. It distinctly still echoes in my ear as I remember him saying this 'You're beautiful,' Blushing, I embraced him. He pulled me down to the edge of the seat with my ass slightly hanging over it. He wrapped his arms around my back and he swung me onto his lap. In one brutal thrust he set me down on his hard HUGE

length, filling me so suddenly that I cried out in shock. His hands roamed, over my back and bottom, on my breasts, rubbing against my nipples. He was everywhere. He pulled me back up then and slammed down again. I completely felt like I was flying, spinning, unsure of where anything even started and ended. Waves of pleasure rolled over me as I came back to back... Click! Click!

It was the most intense pleasure I ever felt in my entire life. What made it more intense was his coming at the same time. My fingers dug into his shoulders. I felt nothing but me and him! If you could hear the grunts I made, you would be embarrassed for me. I was like an animal. But get this, after he came, he was instantly hard again... what the hell, I thought as he started thrusting into me again really fast. It was hot, the windows cracked in the truck we were in. The air was stifling. That sweet scent of sex permeated throughout. There was not a breeze in the *air. I couldn't believe it was possible, but all of a sudden, I had two more orgasms, Click! Click! just before James was able to come a second time. When I finally felt myself coming back down to earth, I clung to him as his now flaccid penis and all of our juices gushed out. I reached down and took some of it and began rubbing my clitoris and oh my goodness, another one - Click!*

I clung to him, kissing his face and neck. The last part I remember as I pulled back was that he gave me a sultry glare, with a satisfied smile on his lips. 'There will NEVER be anyone better! EVER!' he shouted. His breathing was heavy and exhausted. That was the most amazing thing a man has ever said to me!"

Charlene literally relived the story as she told it to the girls who sat living the experience vicariously through her. She didn't share with them that she had just had an orgasm telling that story. *Click!* A couple of the girls themselves did not reveal that they too were having mild orgasms, but had you looked around the room you may have noticed.

Irene looked at Charlene in disbelief. She tried to visualize these crazy positions. She felt like Charlene was talking this provocative sexual stuff because it made her more interesting. Charlene had always had this insatiable need for attention. Irene threw Charlene some shade. She wasn't buying this claim of forty-eight orgasms in forty hours. Irene was overly sexual and she herself couldn't boast of anything as dynamic as that. The doorbell rang, taking the chill out of the room.

Yanique LaCroix pulled up in her brand new black BMW 7 series. Her settlement was doing her well. Of the three million dollars she received because of that asshole doctor, she donated one hundred thousand to Haiti, she moved to the Summerlin area of Las Vegas, where her girlfriends were, and purchased a new house for her mom and her daughters. Dr. Benoit had set the boundaries, but she had won the game.

She missed her gals. She was happy to be joining them for Charlene's bachelorette party. She rang the doorbell. Kim opened the door and let her in. "Oh my God, look who the cat dragged in!" All of the girls were happy to see her and as girls do, they screamed and welcome her with loving arms. They had missed her. Each had their own personal relationship with Yanique and valued her friendship although every one of them thought she was crazy as hell. She had, after all, been diagnosed borderline bi-polar. The girls gathered around Yanique bombarding her with questions about what had been going on in her life.

"Ladies this is Charlene's gala. She is the life of *this* party! I will fill you all in on what other boundaries I may have crossed since the Dr. Benoit situation." She handed Kim two bottles of Patron. "Charlene, let's get your party going girl!"

Chapter Four

Kathy Wilson looked over at Theresa and smiled. She wondered if she recognized her. She was pleasantly surprised to see her at this wedding party.

Kathy and Theresa had met long ago when they were in their early twenties. In fact, she remembered going to her apartment and getting a book from her called Our Bodies Ourselves. She wondered how many other women Theresa handed out that book to. It was actually a health book designed to make her feel more comfortable with her own body.

For some reason Theresa had been very easy to talk to. This was a girl who asked her own mother if she engaged in oral sex. Can you imagine asking your mother a question like that? And then imagine your mother responding with, "I don't like having it done, but I like doing it." Wow! Kathy's own mother had told her *Don't ever let a man go down on you. They will suck your insides out.'* She literally meant that. So began Kathy's life of sexual anxiety.

Kathy decided to take her boyfriend with her. Steve was a good provider. He was a mailman who put in a lot of hours and had bought a gorgeous house for them to share.

They weren't married and he was beginning to feel like all he was good for was being a provider. He loved her and didn't want to be unfaithful, but the sex was just the epitome of the meaning of Wham Bam thank you ma'am.

Most of the time Kathy would just lie there and let him do his thing. At times she would wake up and find him in her. For him it didn't matter if she was asleep or awake. Either way it was like making love to a corpse.

And the day he did try to have oral sex with her, to please her, he asked her to scream out if it felt good. She pretended she had felt something that made her feel good and shouted with as much enthusiasm as she could muster, *"Okay daddy! Suck my pee-pee hole! Suck my pee-pee hole!"*

What damn grown woman said those words? He was sickened. Maybe he should get out of this relationship. There was nothing binding him to her other than his feelings. In all other aspects she was a good woman. She pleased him in every other way.

Kathy didn't get out the house much. She had been in an abusive marriage at a young age. Her friends were cautious with her and they never discussed sex because she always responded as if it was taboo. But Theresa had been an exception. She didn't even remember how they met, but Theresa was very open and talked to her about how she loved having a man go down on her.

It took a lot out of Kathy to ask Theresa if she had ever returned the favor and gave oral sex to a guy. She had admonished Kathy that she would lose Steve if she didn't start sucking his dick or being a little more creative even in allowing him to perform cunnilingus, a word she couldn't even pronounce and sounded disgusting to her.

After all of their conversations, when she went to pick up the book, she decided to take Steve along with her. It was like this girl was going to be their sex therapist. Steve was very open in front of her. It made Kathy a bit uneasy.

And now here she was at fifty-five still in a state of arrested development. She just couldn't bring herself to change.

But one thing Theresa was wrong about, Steve was still by her side. She thought he would have left her by now, particularly the day he said, "Every time I touch you it disgust me." He still came home every night. She would be obligatory whenever he wanted to make love to her, yet accusatory whenever he wanted to try something new.

"Where did you learn that from? Who taught you that?" she would ask. She had never caught him cheating in all these years.

By accusing him of cheating, it would eliminate his desire to try to add some spice into their non-existent love life. She just hadn't wanted to be bothered. *Ever.*

Chapter Five

"Theresa, what happened between you and Vincent? Did you ever get to fuck him again?" Charlene asked, yelling across the room, "Hell girl, talked about was that damn 'Magic' so much it made me want to fuck him!"

Terri surfaced momentarily bursting into hysterical laughter. Theresa told the story as quickly as she could as each girl sat attentively. She didn't want to dominate the evening. This was Charlene's night. So she gave them a quick sneak peek into what happened after she wrote Obsessions raising everyone's interest even further as she ended with, "Well, he could have told me he had a fake penis."

"Well, what did you expect him to say?" chimed Wendy, "Excuse me while I pump up my dick!"

The room erupted with laughter, almost bringing many of the girls to tears.

The night went on with the girls sharing their most unique orgasms.

"Whew, one time I had this orgasm and I thought I was going to lose my mind. There was this guy named Nathan. He first simply started licking my clitoris and it started sticking out as if it was a penis. He then took my labia lips and stretched it with his lips and used my lips to cover over my clitoris completely wrapping it tight, as if tucking it into a shell. But because it was erect, it was so snug and that pressure itself gave way to an awesome feeling.

I don't know how he managed, but he held it like that and started sucking on it. I went crazy. I was wiggling and screaming like there was no tomorrow. It was truly overwhelming and then my body locked up and I went into spasms, giving way to the biggest orgasm I ever had. Hell, I was a ball of orgasms because I was shaking and shaking. Probably was really just twenty seconds, but it certainly felt longer. I didn't want it to stop.

I was in my early thirties when I had that one. I don't know if he just got lucky with that technique because I haven't been able to have that duplicated to this day!"

All the girls were feeling the throbbing in their own bodies after hearing that story. "Oh my God," moaned Jessica her voice somewhat raspy as if she herself was going to come right at that moment, "That sounds so damn good. Why are we talking about this?"

"Hey, we want Charlene to have another forty eight! And we want to learn some stuff too! Never hurts to get some new game," responded Irene, still skeptical of Charlene's claim to forty eight orgasms in forty hours.

"Right. Right," said Jessica, "Honestly, I want to leave right now to go try it out on my girlfriend."

The others were feeling the same. Kathy sat enviously. She had never experienced anything like that.

But hey, let the pajama party continue.

As the evening went on they continued to share stories, but stopped to open gifts. Of course her sofa was adorned with the Victoria Secrets negligees, and someone even bought an obligatory Crock Pot.

Charlene pretty much had everything. She and Nick had been living together for quite a few years before she agreed to marry him. Her favorite gift however, came surprisingly from Marja who designed a special gift basket from Bedroom Kandi. Charlene wasn't too familiar with the brand but she knew it came from a celebrity on one of those Housewives' shows.

She had met Marja and Wendy at a construction company she worked for where the boss was a major asshole. The boss had always given Marja so much credit as if she could do no wrong, Charlene found herself resenting her. She never expected her to show up at her bridal shower, let alone give her the best gift of all!

Chapter Six

Finally the stripper arrived. Some of the girls were on pins and needles waiting for his arrival. Some of them weren't interested. Most of them were heading into their late forties. They had seen enough dancing scrotums and dicks flopping around.

They needed something a little different. Sharing the secrets of their orgasms was enough for them. They were getting horny and couldn't wait to try some of these things on their significant others.

Kathy, Victoria and Jessica found their way into the dining room where the food was. Kathy didn't want to look at another man's body when she could barely look at Steve's. The three ladies decided they would sit this dancer out. They had to cool themselves down anyway from the stories they had already heard!

Chapter Seven

Kim walked over and opened the door. "Hold it ladies, Irene ordered the obligatory surprise for the evening. He is a hotty."

Although seemingly older than what the woman were accustomed to, his package was complete. His face resembled that of Johnny Depp. His dark brown hair parted down the center and fell to his face. A medium thick mustache sat over his small lips and a really small goatee lined the under lips. He was a tall man. His stomach an eight pack. He had a tight ass along with thighs beyond those of steel. He certainly had a lot of flavor. He sarcastically went by the name of Little Joe. But his manhood was larger than most.

Kim fanned herself as she walked him into the den of these sinful women. Wait, she laughed to herself, "I'm one of them!" She took a sip of her Long Island Ice tea. Her second one of the evening. Good thing this is a sleepover.

Victoria had not expected this kind of a party at all. She had anticipated the stripper and the usual game playing that goes on at these girlie types of events. She had known Charlene all of her life and ever since she had this illicit affair with James she had changed quite a bit.

Chapter Eight

Little Joe started his first dance to the tune of Def Leppard called Pour Some Sugar On Me. He singled out Lorraine to dance with him. She moved her body sexily, slinking her body over his dick and dropping it cause it *was* hot, showing all the gals she still had what it takes to get the job done. "Go Rainbow! Go Rainbow!" the girls sang encouragingly.

After two songs, sweat dripped down his body. He glistened, looking even more sexy. The loud music flowed throughout the house, the bass causing things to rattle.

"Take a break Little Joe before you give Charlene her private dance." Irene told him.

They moved a chair into the middle of the room and sat Charlene in it. They adorned her in a Queen's crown and sash. All of the women had been required to wear sexy lingerie and Charlene made sure hers was easy to take off. She decided she would strip down with the stripper and let loose. When he starts to dance for her, she would surprise them and instead dance with him. She would strip down to her panties. That was her plan. Again, after all, she was the queen of orgasms. Hey, maybe I'll let them see me coming!

Charlene started reminiscing back to her last night with James. James had gotten her a luxurious suite at the Marriott Hotel. She was almost in tears that her trip was coming to a close. She would hold these orgasms in her frontal lobe memory forever. She picked up the clicker off the dresser. She was astonished when she looked at the number. Whew forty-six orgasms! That's crazy. She knew once she went home, there wouldn't even be any sex.

James had to go home last night. It poked at Charlene just a tad bit as she wondered if he fucked his wife. She shook the thought out of her head. It's all about me right now. It's all that mattered. She would be marrying Nick soon anyway.

She greeted James at the door in a white satin robe straight from Victoria's Secret. She had showered and put on her favorite perfume - Chanel No 5 - a throwback classic. There was not a necessity for words. She let her robe slide to the floor. His eyes widened. She felt sexy. She removed his shirt showing his chiseled physique. Long deep kisses dominated as he led her to the bed. His breath was hot and hungry. He cradled her as he kicked off his jeans and settled the length of his body against hers.

This time he was being more tender. He gently traced the areola of her breast and then began traveling his hands downward causing her abdomen to collapse into her spine. He massaged her shoulders and gave soft lip bites on her lower neck. He kissed her in the most intimate regions of her body, providing short nibbles on her clitoris. Perspiration sheened her skin as that ache begged to be released. It didn't take long for a cascading wave to ripple through her body. Click! She bucked upward, wanting more. James didn't disappoint. He gently thrust inside of her as she gasped, holding him tightly. She kissed the spot where his neck joined his shoulder muscles. He groaned, moving faster and deeper. When she felt they were both close, particular herself, she reached over and grabbed her small dildo, favorite sex toy of hers, off of the night stand. She took the gadget and turned it on. James noticed the sound of it and smiled approvingly. She opened her legs widely and lifted them up in the air. She took the dildo and inserted it just into of her bottom hole. The sensation of James within her as she stimulated her own ass, started both their bodies to shaking, bringing them both to massive orgasms to the point of total completeness. Forty-Eight! Click!

Waking up from her memories, Charlene, flustered and wet, was truly ready for her dance. Little Joe stood up but before he could start the music Irene stood up. "Excuse me ladies," she said as she walked across the room in her black and red laced teddy revealing her slender figure that she worked out every day to maintain.

"I would like to suggest a DARE! All this time we have been giving truth and telling our unique orgasms. Little Joe here is a, well, to put it nicely a gigolo. I paid for him! He is here for our pleasure. So Charlene," Irene hesitated, "I dare you to have one of your forty-eight orgasms in front of us!"

Irene was smug and stood smiling actually holding up Little Joe's penis. It stood straight and rigid in her hand.

Irene got the reaction she was expecting. Kim shook her head in disbelief, but couldn't leave the room. The other ladies, most of them horny from the stories, couldn't bring themselves to move. Surely, they would watch. But they could not participate.

"Don't do it Charlene," quietly warned Yanique, "Don't do that shit in front of your gals. You will lose their respect." Yanique was unaware that some of the girls had already lost it.

Charlene was completely thrown off guard. She was being challenged by a bitch she didn't even like. Irene was trying to steal her thunder. So she would accept the challenge just on that merit alone.

"Well," she responded nervously, "Hmphf, as the queen of orgasms and by tomorrow I will be married and totally off limits, I accept this dare. I want you all to witness my cremation... get it! Cream... get it." Her laughter was weak.

The room was full of nervous energy. Irene started the sultry music of Joe Cocker's, You Can Keep Your Hat On as Little Joe sauntered over to Charlene, "Lie back in the chair and spread eagle," he ordered. She did as she was told while the other girls watched on.

Charlene had chosen sexy lingerie that was easy to remove. The ladies sat, eyes wide, their mouths ajar in disbelief at what was about to happen. She was going to fuck this man in front of them. It was too much for most of them. Voyeurism with permission. They couldn't turn their heads.

As soon as Little Joe put his tongue on her leg and started moving slowly up her leg, she began to feel aroused, but suddenly Charlene jumped up out of the chair. "I can't... I can't..." She may have been able to do this in private, but in front of her friends, no way.

"Just as I thought," teased Irene, "Orgasm Queen wimp!" She walked over to the chair and gently pushed Charlene onto the floor and the sat her ass in Charlene's position on the chair, spreading herself eagle.

Charlene, in slight shock, picked herself up and grabbed the glass of wine she had sat on the table and threw it at her.

Irene didn't respond. Little Joe would be all she was going to respond to tonight. In fact, maybe he could lick it off. The thought increased her excitement.

The music had stopped and there was complete silence in the room. Funny thing is Charlene found herself wanting to watch. She put aside the anger and got comfortable. Kim handed her a shot of Patron.

Yanique grabbed the corner of the couch to steady herself as she pulled her cell phone out of her bra. No way was she going to let this Worldstar action go on without documentary.

With Little Joe straddling over her, Irene sat up and reached for him and grabbed him towards her. He steadied himself with the chair's edge to keep from falling.

Irene began sucking his nipples with a lot of pressure causing a pleasurable pain making him cry out. He always loved it when the 'John' played an active role. She then pushed him away and ordered him to sit straddled in the chair. Irene loved being in control. She tweaked his nipples again, which assured her an unceasingly hard, rigid dick. She positioned herself over him. Without warning, she slammed her pussy down hard on top of his dick to make sure he would fill it up. Each up and down motion became harder and harder. It was her rodeo and he was the cowboy. Each downward motion hit her G spot. The rougher it was, the better it felt for her. Both she and Little Joe hollered loud words in ecstasy which definitely were not terms of endearment. "Fuck! That feels so damn good!" shouted Irene her voice raspy. "Come on baby slam that shit on me. Get it all in there." Little Joe encouraged. Her heart rate rose. Her muscles tensed and her lungs filled with oxygen. Click! Click! Her eyes dilated as two back to back orgasms brought her trembling to her knees

Half the girls were feeling embarrassed, the others wanted to join in. Kim turned around and whispered to Theresa, "The way Irene is coming down on that dick, I bet Irene is into that dominatrix shit." Theresa just sat continuing to watch. She was amazed Irene was still that versatile for her age.

Irene was always boisterous in her lovemaking. Although Little Joe was getting paid, she was pro-active in her acts and reciprocated the desires and was making Little Joe scream out. He enjoyed every second with sexually responsive women and making money at the same time. *That* he felt was the beauty of this job!

Irene wasn't finished. She lifted herself off of him and had him get up from the chair. She positioned herself hands down on it. Little Joe approached her from behind, leaning over and rubbing her breast and returning the favor by pinching the nipples hard. He learned that women sometimes do to him what they wanted done to themselves. He entered her slowly at first. He began picking up the pace, slapping her ass with each thrust. Suddenly, they were distracted by a woman's scream. Did one of the girls want to join in?

The wild yelling and the moaning echoed straight into the earshot of the three girls in the dining room. Suddenly Kathy seemed to recognize the familiarity of the male voice, "What the hell is going on in there?" the girls wondered as Victoria and Jessica rushed up out of their seats to see what was happening.

Kathy sat frozen. The familiarity of the male's voice pierced through her soul. "No," she said astonished, "Can't possibly be! It just can't possibly be!" She continued to mumble those words as his voice became more clear. She could recognize Steve's voice anywhere.

A tight knot grew in her stomach as rage built up within her. When the knot burst, Kathy grabbed a knife off the table and ran wildly into the living room. Her breathing was heavy. Her eyes widened in insanity. Looking like a madwoman from Psycho, when her eyes witnessed Steve's, penis pummeling up and down in Irene, with the knife securely in hand, Kathy ran over and began stabbing both of them, aiming for nowhere in particular. Blood gushed everywhere.

Everyone was too shocked to respond instantly until Yanique and Charlene reacted by grabbing her and holding her down. They used all their strength to hold her as her arms flailed wildly about. Jessica called 911.

Yanique examined her arm as blood dripped down it. It was just a surface scratch. She shook her head, laughing sarcastically, "And they say *I'm* the crazy one."

Irene was stunned when she looked up and saw Kathy coming at her with a butcher knife. She froze. The eroticism of the moment eroded quickly as the knife blinded her eyes. It seemed an eternity before she tried to jump out of the way. Kathy managed to stab her several times. She was taken to the hospital with no major arteries having been hit. She would miss the wedding. Neither she nor Charlene would regret that.

Kathy had never known Steve was a male prostitute. She couldn't believe her eyes when she witnessed his penis going in and out of another woman. But what had made her more upset was that he was giving this woman the orgasms she wasn't able to experience herself. She had lived for years with a man she had never truly known. She had thought the love he had for her kept him away from other women and that his physical desire for sex had died out. She was totally mistaken.

Steve had tried with Kathy for years to make something of their sex life. He wanted the intensity of a great orgasm instead of what she offered. He did truly love her so instead of finding a woman for an affair that he didn't want to emotionally find himself vested in. He chose financial gain by offering himself for sale.

He had been living this life for several years. He had started out hiring call girls. It was their candidness that made him realize the need in the industry for male escorts. He had never realized the lucrativeness of male escorts in Las Vegas. Women were normally out to get the money, not pay for it.

Kathy seldom went to any kind of party. If she left the house, it was to go to her parents' house. He never expected her to be with this group of women and never anticipated getting caught, let alone getting stabbed. It was all going so smoothly and he still had his day job. In either job he was delivering something, he joked aimlessly to himself. As he lay on the gurney, bleeding profusely, he wondered what would become of them.

Victoria picked up her cell phone and called Michael. She realized now what was lacking within her. Her lack of sexual energy had actually pushed him away. Was it so bad looking at porn movies? She could clearly answer that question after the stories she heard this evening. It would take some time, but she had to get her sexy on. She was leaving with some great ideas. Yes, she was smiling. These orgasms sounded delicious. Why had she allowed herself to miss these feelings? She was going to change that. Fortunately, for both of them, they still communicated constantly and he remained unattached. A mischievous smiled adorned her face.

Michael had not answered the phone. She left a message and then sent him a text – 'Hey big boy, how about you come over and fuck me tonight!' She knew coming from her that would make his mouth drop.

The click of the handcuffs on Kathy's wrist brought her out of her state of madness. She had snapped. She had come to this party hoping to loosen up. She felt Steve had been getting restless. What man stays with a woman for all these years when that woman doesn't have sex with him? He in no way let on he was cheating. Or perhaps he didn't consider it cheating. It was a job. He was a damn male prostitute. It was beyond her comprehension.

Chapter Nine

Although the drama of the orgasm revelations and the attempted murder that took place forty-eight hours earlier were still fresh in their minds, the wedding would go on as scheduled. The girls had been temporarily rattled, but they easily shook it off since no one had gotten seriously hurt. They were more disappointed about not getting more orgasm techniques. "We can always have another party," suggested Yanique. "The party was just getting started!"

Forty-eight white, fire flickering, tea light candles lined the pews. There were twenty-four on each side. As Charlene slowly walked down the aisle, she counted them. An unhappy smile lit her face as she approached her soon to be husband, her destiny.

As she counted the last candle, she was reminded of the extraordinary forty-eight orgasms she oozed out during that four day fling. This was something she knew she would never achieve with her husband. It was at that moment, she truly realized she was subscribing to a life of unsatisfying sex. It would be a marriage devoid of romance and affection.

Perhaps, just perhaps, she will seek out James just one more time.

The champagne glasses were raised! *Click!*

Forty-eight days later, she filed for divorce.

The End

About the Author

Theresa J. Gonsalves was born November 24, 1958.

She currently has published the following books:

Obsessions (Adult non-fiction)

The Man in the Woods (Adult fiction)

Remember the Time (Specialty non-fiction)

Eating Gavin's Way (Children)

Eating Azure's Way (Children)

....*more to come soon!*